Seven from
Heaven

Cecelia,

"Amani na Upendo"

Peace a Love

J. Cullis

Also by John Anthony Cullis:

Anna Carsen: Journey to Joy

SEVEN FROM HEAVEN

A Biography of a Bantu Slave

1790 - 1860

by

JOHN ANTHONY CULLIS

published by

CT Publishing Company

CT Publishing Company
2636 Churn Creek Road
Redding, CA 96002

© 1996 by John Anthony Cullis

Library of Congress Catalog Card Number: 96-84881

ISBN 1-56226-288-2

ACKNOWLEDGMENT

I wish to express deep appreciation to my son Brian who took time from his doctoral research to type my handwritten manuscript, my daughter Monica for her proofreading and lastly to thank my wife for giving me her work space!

Cover Design by Bob Whelchel

TABLE OF CONTENTS

PROLOGUE

JOHNSTOWN, PENNSYLVANIA, 1860
Monday, October 2, 1860

*F*rom the window of my second story newspaper office, I view Central Park, the heart of our city. Today it is practically void of people as a cold, drizzling rain washes the variegated leaves of their dust and grime. An early frost has announced the beginning of autumn and an overcast sky has added a foreboding touch.

Normally, the park and its people are an inspiration for my daily human interest column but on a dark, depressive day such as this, my heart and my head both seem empty. Even the office, lighted by high hanging chandeliers, is nearly deserted. Only a copy boy, the porter and I are on duty; the rest of the staff are about town seeking interesting items for tomorrow's *Cambria Tribune*. I purposely had my desk turned to face the window so I could sit as a single audience and watch the actors on the stage across the street and somehow perhaps glean a story.

My reverie is broken by a rough, guttural "Harumph" from the stair landing. James M. Swank, publisher, critic and associate owner of the newspaper with Mr. John Brown stood there attired in his black derby, rain slicker and brogans. He noisily clomped his wet squishing brogans and Irish Black Thorn cane across the bare wooden floor to my desk and without a word, grabbed the chair from the adjoining desk and plopped into the seat.

"John and I have uncovered a story accidentally and we believe you are the right man for the assignment," he added. "When you hear it, we believe you'll be just as enthused about it as we are."

My interest peaked as he continued. "There's a runaway slave living up the valley along Hinkston Run behind the Cambria Iron Works. This is no ordinary man. He stands seven feet two inches tall and weighs three hundred pounds; a black giant among us! He's kind, altruistic, intelligent in a philosophical way and adheres to strict Christian principles. Despite the horrible, wretched life he endured as a slave, he appears to bear no bitterness toward anyone.

Fred Krebs from over at the mill tells us that he was hired by his foreman to work at the coke ovens and that gave him a grubstake to build a house and settle down with his wife at the junction of Hinkston Run and Benchoff Hill Roads.

Now I want you to go up there first thing in the morning and strike a deal. We'll give him seven hundred dollars for exclusive rights to his life story. Drop everything else you're doing and concentrate on this man's biography. Gain his trust so he can be completely open and candid with you. The money would mean a great deal of security for him and his wife.

We'll run a full page serial on him once a week. It should increase circulation if we print it on different days of the week so the public will buy the paper to follow the story. Talk of slavery is a big issue these days in Washington and I have a hunch Lincoln is about to abolish it. This man's story will give the abolitionists something to chew on. Get on it and give it all you've got."

Though the story intrigued me, I couldn't help asking, "What if he doesn't want to divulge his past; what if he fears being caught and returned?"

"I know he doesn't have much," my boss replied. "And I think the offer of so much money might be appealing to him. He's a friendly and affable man. I really don't think he fears very much of anything or anyone."

I had my assignment and Mr. Swank's final instructions. "Don't waste my time with negative hypothetical possibilities. Get your briefcase ready, prepare a contract and put the proposition to him. I'll be by in a few days to read your first serial. Do a good job and if we like it, Brownie and I have agreed to give you a bonus. This story should increase our circulation by the hundreds. I'll be back."

By eight the next morning, I was first in line at the Washington Street Livery Stable to rent their young high-spirited gray Morgan and a lightweight business buggy. Ten minutes later I was heading west, crossing the canal and newly laid railroad tracks. We sure were proud of our new railroad from the east connecting us to Pittsburgh. This will spell the end for the canal although barges were still running to Blairsville. The railroad will deliver passengers faster and cheaper.

I trotted past the blast furnace and the coke ovens and took the road to the right up along Hinkston Run. Fog was still rolling off Prospect Hill and the dew was heavy in the air sticking to my jacket like tiny beads of glass. The Morgan was feeling her oats this beautiful, colorful fall morning keeping a fast rhythmic trot up the serpentine road toward Wesley Chapel.

About two miles down the road I noticed a small, neat cottage on the left. Smoke was rising from the chimney. There was a split rail fence enclosing a patch of green lawn and a sleek Bay mare grazing off to the side. Not until I pulled up to the gate did I notice the large dark man sitting on the porch, puffing a homemade corncob pipe with a tether in his hand attached to the Bay.

The cottage was simple but neat, made of large home-made brick. A porch stuck out six feet supported by four locust posts furnished with a bench to the left of the door and a very large homemade Morris chair, wired together to the right of the door. The huge man sat stoically on the bench with his eyes fixed upon me with an apprehensive gaze. All runaways were vigilant for bounty hunters so their caution was understandable.

"Good morning," I announced with a smile. "May I have a word with you?"

"Yes suh" he answered in a deep southern accent. "Do you come in peace?"

"Oh, most assuredly," I said apologetically, for I didn't want to frighten him. "I come on a mission of friendship with a proposal that I hope will interest you. My name is Jack Zane and I'm a reporter for the *Cambria Tribune*. My boss is willing to pay you seven hundred dollars for your life's story."

"For my story, what story is that? I ain't got no story, man. Are you jossing me or sumpin?"

"My paper would like to hear your life's story from the day you were born right down to this very morning today. Do you understand?"

A beautiful warm smile lighted his round chocolate face. He pushed his sweat stained hat to the back of his head and chuckled, "Man this is the most crazy talk I heard of and you all say you'll give me seven hundred dollars and I hafta do nothing but sit here and jaw?"

"That's the agreement," I responded with a broad grin. "Just give us your signature on this contract to print your story, no small print and no strings attached to deceive you."

"Jenny, Jenny! Come out here a minit. Come hear what this man say!"

A very attractive tan woman with shoulder-length ebony hair came out on the porch. She was about my height, six feet, and as slim and trim a woman as I've ever seen. She seemed to be about sixty-five years old. Her freshly laundered print apron over a flowered housecoat told me she was a meticulously neat housekeeper. Her husband related my offer to her and her eyes widened to show more white than brown.

"Land sakes," she uttered. "That's the most money we both have all our lives. I can't believe it. I just can't!"

"By the way, sir, my name is Ben. Ben David. My slave name was Dolt Jowers, my owner's name. But now I call myself Ben David. It means mighty in spirit, and David's my hero in the Bible."

"Ben, I'm curious. Why do you hold on to that rope? Why don't you just tie it to the porch post?," I asked.

"He, he, he," he laughed. "Supposin' a rabbit or varmint was to run out and spook my horse? There'd go my porch. Understand?"

"I've been a city boy all my life so I have a lot to learn about practical matters and I'm wagering that before I have completed your story, I'll have an education that a college couldn't give. If it is all alright with you, we'll start our story writing the first thing tomorrow morning. Now if you just sign your name to this agreement giving us exclusive rights to your life's story, I'll be on my way."

6

"I'll hafta sign in print for I ain't learned to write nice in script yet, but I'm practicing. My real name was Kaka Zuri. That means handsome brother in Swahili. When bad people take you, they take your name too."

"That all will be put in your story tomorrow. I will want to know you as well as you know yourself. I'll want to know what you feel inside; what your philosophy of life is."

He pulled himself up off the bench and stood like a giant towering above me. He appeared to be more like eight feet tall.

"What I am is all inside, this outside shell means nothing. I've got da good Lord in here," pointing to his huge chest.

"That's the story I'm after, Ben," I said excitedly. "I want to know where, when and how you were born, what you did, how you felt, what others did to you and how you responded to it all. What brought you to Johnstown and how you survived. This story will take time but I'll be as expedient and prompt as possible. I'll be taking your story down in Pitman shorthand."

"I'll have my chores done and awaiting for you in da morning," he promised in his deep rich bass voice.

"Then I'll head back to the office and prepare for tomorrow." I thanked Mrs. David graciously for her hospitality and departed. I turned my rig around and headed for town, keeping the Morgan down to a fast walk. I needed this time to think, for this is going to be my best piece of journalism. I'll call it my 'piece de resistance.'

In the many interviews I held in my career, I found most people tend to withdraw and clam up when they know what they say will be read by thousands, but this assignment will be different. Ben appears to be open, honest and unpretentious so my interview should flow easily. Our readers will be able to glide through his life's story in constant anticipation and interest. I'll want to keep the richness of his accent yet paraphrase his story so as to make it comprehensible.

My mind had been so preoccupied that I found myself at the junction of Mill and Furnace Streets before I realized it. I returned the rig with the understanding that it be reserved for me for the next two weeks, including Sunday. Ben was seventy years old and I didn't want to take any chances of losing this story.

■■■■■■■■■■

*T*he sun would not be up for another half hour when I loaded my brief case, lap writing desk and lunch into the buggy, waved to the stable boy and headed out the valley to Ben's. I felt like a poor reporter who had just won the lottery, for I had a sure winner. The winner of the Cambria lottery was set up for life and that's how I felt— exhilarated!

Ben was leaning against the porch post wearing faded blue bib overalls with his old hat sitting precariously on the back of his head as I approached the brick cottage. He gave me a big wave with his long arms reaching to the porch eaves. His broad grin told me that he was anxious to get started on his seven hundred dollar windfall.

"Morning, Mr. Jack," his deep voice breaking the morning silence. "Let's put your horse back yonder in the grass for the day with my mare. Plenty of feed there."

"That would be just dandy," I responded. "I left in such a hurry that I plumb forgot her nose bag of oats."

By the time Ben returned to the front porch, I had my lap desk set up and my note pad and pencil all ready. He pulled his stool over next to the Morris chair and plumped down with his back to the wall. The thud brought Jenny out the door. "Morning Mr. Jack. How are you all today?"

"Just fine, Ma'am," I answered. "I hope we don't disturb you and interfere with your work."

"No, sir. Not at all. I'll keep outa your way," she replied.

"Oh, one thing more I might add, Ben. I will be rewriting your story with different wording. It will be what you say, only reworded. I will not change the content one bit. Is that alright with you? We call it paraphrasing."

"Yes, sir. That's good. My talk is not so good like yours."

"How did you learn English, Ben, since you never went to school?," I asked.

"I learned what I could on my own, but I got real teaching from Aunt Mae. She taught me reading and printing and simple numbers. I can add, subtract, multiply and do some fractions. I owe Aunt Mae a great debt."

"We'll get all this in the story, Ben. Now let's start at the beginning when you were born."

BEN DAVID: A SLAVE'S OWN STORY

CAMBRIA TRIBUNE
Tuesday, October 10, 1860
FIRST DAY STORY

Editor's Note: The following biography of an African slave was personally told to me word for word. Due to his limited vocabulary and southern accent, I will relay to you in the vernacular. As he attempts to search for a word to convey his thoughts, I will assist him by using an appropriate word. I will use this substitution as rarely as possible so as not to dilute its authenticity. Once each week I will devote a full page to his biography until his life's story is told in full. The graphic illustrations are done by Jan Flaugh. Read and enjoy.

–Jack Zane

I was born Kaka Zuri, which means "handsome brother," about the year 1790 on the east coast of Africa. My people were Zulu of the Bantu tribe who migrated south from the Rufiji river region. We were a mixture of Negroid and Arab blood who spoke Swahili which means "coast people." We were light skinned and much taller than neighboring tribes, therefore we were easily recognized when interspersed with others.

My family were farmers and our whole clan lived in a kraal (village) making us all blood relatives. The father of my mother's father was the shaman of our kraal and it was he who told us of our heritage and Nilotic ancestry.

From as long as I can remember, I was trained to be a tracker and hunter so that when I grew up I could provide meat for our kraal. My name was changed to Ubingwa Mwindaji which meant "skilled hunter" in hopes that I would grow up to honor my name. I was taught to read the ground and the sky, the grass and wind and all that anyone else might believe to be insignificant. Nothing was too small to overlook.

We were a peaceful and contented people who shared everything on a communal basis for one blood flowed through all of us. My cousin Kaidi, which means "headstrong" and I were of the same age so we spent all our time together honing our skills. We were strong and muscular for we ran great distances and climbed trees so high that the animals could not detect our scent. We were both obedient to our parents and respected them for that was how they were raised. My parents never hesitated to show their love for us nor did our aunts and uncles. We were truthful and trusting and that is what led to our downfall.

One early spring day in my tenth year, a very large dhow (square-rigged boat) sailed into our harbor from the North. Five men and two women came into our kraal. The men were Arab and the women black. They brought fruit, sugar-filled dates for all the children, and a strong fermented drink for the adults. They said they came in peace as friends and wished to fill their casks with fresh water. My great-grandfather welcomed them so we joined together to eat, drink and dance.

I had never witnessed a celebration that lasted so long for at sunset the drink was affecting the adults and they had a difficult time dancing to the drums. When night fell, the two women gathered us children, about twenty, and took us aboard the dhow for it would be impossible for us to sleep in our kibandas with all the noise. We were led below deck in a room dimly lighted by a single oil lamp. The eerie shadows cast on the walls of the room and the strong smell of millet gave all of us a sense of apprehension. We could see sacks of millet piled about the room and could feel the dhow slowly sway putting us all in a dreamy state. The women asked us to lay on the sacks and try to sleep to the rhythm of the boat. We trusted them.

When we awoke we could see daylight through the cracks of the doors overhead and could feel the sea splashing outside the walls and a much greater movement of the boat. I shook Kaidi and told him that we were in open water and far from our kraal. His face first showed fear then rage as he hollered, "Nisaidia, Nisaidia." "Help, Help!" All the other children awakened at his cry and asked what was happening. I told them that we were being kukamata by evil people and they had given our parents kileo that made them drunk.

The room was filled with screaming and crying and Kaidi and I could not quiet them down. A sudden pounding on the door overhead and the command "Kimya, Kimya, Silence, Silence" by a gruff male voice. We all stood in shock not knowing what evil might befall us next, no one uttered a sound. My eight year old cousin Ua Moto came running over to me and wrapped her fragile arms around my waist, sobbing inwardly. The door opened, filling the room with bright light showing a cluster of wet eyed children as frightened as a baby gnu chased by a mother lion.

Two wooden baskets were lowered on a hemp rope, one contained water and the other filled with millet mush. Kaidi and I each unhooked the buckets and the rope was pulled up and the door closed again. We were all blinded for a few minutes and then we set about to plan just as we did when we were going out on a hunt. Everything must first be thought out and a plan devised. Since Kaidi and I were among the oldest and the most experienced in being away from our kraal, we took charge.

Where we were going and how long it would take was unknown. We had to have order and care for one another and that meant dividing the food and water equally. We took count and there were seventeen boys and three girls, two age twelve and one age eight. The girls would do the dividing of water and food and the boys would do what we could to arrange the millet sacks for sleeping and sitting. To pass time, we would take exercise by doing our puberty (ubalehe) dance twice a day and playing word games to keep our minds alert.

Kaidi pounded on the door until one of the women who led us on board answered his knock. He told her that if we did not have a container for our Kinyesi, we would defile and contaminate their cargo of millet. She told us she would fetch one immediately. When she opened the hatch we were momentarily blinded so we were unable to see the half barrel coming down on us. It bounced off the shoulder of Kipawa and then on to the millet. Kipawa winced with pain as he grabbed his shoulder and sank to his knees. I tried to feel for a broken bone but the skin was peeled off and he didn't want me to touch him. I took my portion of warm mush and plastered it over the wound and held it there until it stuck on by itself. He asked me to let him alone, took a drink of water and went over in the corner and laid down.

Kaidi and I had all the others sit down in front of us on the floor and told them our plan to survive. The half barrel would be placed in the far corner and after each one used it we would cover it with two sacks of millet to keep the stench to a minimum. Anyone who wanted to could lead us in a song or even give a speech. Anyone who had any suggestions to keep our spirits high, let them speak out. We will stand for no disagreements for our enemy is only above deck and we here below are all blood relatives.

The days became routine and monotonous as did our daily ration. We extended our mush by adding some raw millet from a sack we opened. At one time we were unable to eat the warm mush for most of us were sick from the pitching and rolling of the ship. When the hatch was opened by a female captor, we asked why the sea was so rough and she said we were rounding the cape. That didn't mean too much to us until we got a sunny day and noticed through the cracks that we changed from a southerly direction to a northerly direction. Then the seas calmed and life was more bearable. Our captors became less suspicious of an escape attempt and permitted us to hand up the barrel of kinyesi and have it emptied. That gave us a breath of fresh air that all took advantage of to the utmost. How good it was!

Looking back those sixty years, I believe we did an outstanding job of surviving. We stressed hope and discouraged despair. Kipawa stayed in a depressed mood the entire voyage for he was in such great pain. He will carry a scar for the rest of his life.

We had a grown-up discussion on the manner we were betrayed by these friendly people from the north. Trust was such an integral part of our lives that we decided it was best to remain trusting since the alternative would be to be cynical. Although I assured them that one day we would return to our old life and village, deep inside I felt we would never see our family again. I feared we would be sold into "utumwa" for we often heard stories of that happening, but only to others. I kept this assumption to myself.

Kipawa moved about holding his right shoulder higher than the other mumbling to himself thoughts of our ultimate fate. Finally he blurted out, "We are all destined to be eaten by our captors. We'll never see our families again." Kaidi and I both overwhelmed him with our shouts. "Upuzi, Upuzi (Nonsense). We are to be used as servants or field hands, we will not be eaten." The other children listened to us for it sounded more plausible and they thought Kipawa might have a fever and be talking out of his head.

By our marks on the bulkhead, we were fourteen days out when the door above us opened and they lowered our buckets of mush and water. After we unhooked them, they withdrew the ropes and lowered a bucket of sheep bones and a bucket of cabbage leaves and orange peelings. It must be a religious holiday for the Arabs and this is the remnants of their feast. We divided the mush equally and then gave the better leaves of cabbage to the girls and gave them their fair share of the orange peelings. For a special treat we took the sheep bones, divided them among us and ate every piece of fat and meat we could glean from the bones. Then we broke them open and sucked the morrow out of every bit down to the tiniest pieces.

That feast was the last good meal we had aboard that floating gereza (prison) for a terrifying storm arose and we were battered from one side of the boat to the other. We restacked the sacks of millet so as to give us a small recess where we could sit together so close that we could not be tossed about.

On the third day of rough weather the woman who lowered our food and water informed us that we were approaching land and this would be our last day aboard. We jumped and laughed, clapping our hands for the stench and the stale air combined with the humidity was the limit that any human could bear.

It was dark when we heard all the activity on deck above us and we would feel the boat slow down and we were in peaceful waters. The thump of the boat coming into the dock threw us all off balance and we were thrown to the deck. Strange voices chattering in a strange language told us we were in a foreign land and our lives would be transferred into merciless and unsympathetic hands.

We sat about in total darkness discussing the possibilities of our new captors being more like our own Bantu people. We imagined all sorts of weird probabilities with an optimistic slant. Eventually one by one we drifted off to sleep, completely exhausted.

The thumping of many feet on the deck overhead brought us all to our senses and we could see sunlight through the cracks of the hatch cover. Suddenly the cover was thrown open and we were flooded by the bright sunlight. A turbaned bearded Arab motioned us to come up the ladder one by one. Kaidi went first, Ua Moto next and then myself. The Arab threw a loop around our necks as each of us came on deck but the greatest shock was to feel the fresh morning air, the sight of a bustling town and all the deep black people milling about. Finally we were all on deck connected by a long hemp rope with the bitter end held by a dirty bearded seedy looking Arab with evil, bloodshot eyes. We were all ordered to take off our nguo and pile them on a barrel head, then two black workers with buckets scooped up sea water and dashed us with the cold chilling "Maji." Despite its breath-taking effect, we were grateful to get the dirt and sweat washed off our bodies. We were born and raised next to the water as we washed clean every day and also learned to swim expertly.

We dried quite readily in the hot sun and were taken aback when the women who gave us our daily ration of food now handed each of us a clean shuka (loincloth). Boys and girls alike. Our attitudes were enlivened as we were marched down a rickety gang plank, across a road crowded with peddlers and vendors who interrupted their business to stop and stare at this coffle of children of yellow cast. The disheveled Arab led us into a building crowded with black men but in the front where we were led sat a row of men in colorful hats and robes. These were chieftains of various tribes who came to outbid one another for our bodies. We all felt like young animals who were less than human.

White people have no idea what it is like to stand on a platform and look down on ten lecherous, greedy chieftains backed by eighty to one hundred tribesmen. It cannot be compared to a group of orphans lined up in a neat row for viewing by prospective parents. We felt like young animals snatched from our parents and put on the block to be taken by the highest bidder. Death appeared very sweet to us even at that age.

The Arabs tried to sell us as a lot but nobody wanted to take all of us so we were placed in groups of four making five groups. Kaidi and I were the tallest and strongest so we were kept together. They then added Kipawa for he was obviously crippled and then Ua Moto was pushed into us for she was considered less valuable.

Each of the chiefs had a slate and chalk and one had an abacus used to figure the commodity equal to our value. Finally the Arabs accepted an offer after much bartering, adding this and subtracting that until it was agreed that Chief Asmak of the Asante Tribe would be our new owner. He was an ugly man with long grayish hair and a bearded chin. Long hair was to depict wisdom but I believe it was more of a diabolical feature.

CAMBRIA TRIBUNE
Wednesday, October 18, 1860
SECOND DAY STORY

We were crammed into a small two wheel cart pulled by two donkeys, one hitched behind the other. The driver sat up front separated from us by our wooden enclosure. A deep black skinned man in a filthy loincloth clung to the back with a pointed stick in his hand. Our ankles were bound to one another so we couldn't escape if we had wanted to. Besides, the chief followed on his donkey led by an aide.

The sun beat down on us mercilessly as we headed north from the seaport of Axim and we were deprived of food and water until we pulled into the village of Tarkwa in late afternoon. We were so thirsty and famished that we ate the rice and yams just as though we were the animals that they thought us to be. We arrived late at night in a deserted village called Prestea. There we were unloaded and allowed to go kinyesi and then tied to a red ironwood tree. We laid in a circle around the tree on the bare ground after brushing away the larger pebbles. Ua Moto sobbed herself to sleep.

It took us eight days of traveling from early morning till late at night before we arrived at the Asante village near the Tao river. It was located between the river and a village. The name of the village, Bibiani, brought to mind the word "bidi" from my own Swahili language which means to be enslaved legally. Enslaving children convinced me that Asmak was an agent of Ibilisi (Devil). I kept repeating that strange name, Bibiani, so the people called me by that name from then on.

The women of the village led us to a thatched kibanda where they cut our rope shackles and pushed us to the ground. There was the ever present switch in their hand as they shouted at us in their native tongue that we could not understand. When the woman grabbed Ua Moto by the ear and pulled her outside the kibanda, we understood her word for "out." They called her "Poku" and gave Kaidi the name "Kweku" not the least bit interested in our given Swahili names. Kipawa was mostly ignored for his disabled shoulder made him as a maimed animal and of little use.

The village consisted of approximately one hundred thatched huts that surrounded a mud brick structure. The porch was as large as the house and it was on this porch that the chief held his court. His tribe we later learned were constantly attacking neighboring tribes for the purpose of taking captives. They viewed us as weird for all of them were very black with broad noses and we were brown with slender noses and much taller.

Our first job was working in the yam fields and gathering Kola nuts. We had to use metal shovels to build the rows two feet high and plant the yams deep inside. Our work was overseen by a large framed black woman who spoke more with her switch than with her tongue.

One evening, after working since sunrise, I was pulling a heavily laden cart of seed yams down a row when I felt the sting of the switch across my back. "Harakisha" she shouted at me. That means hurry up in my native tongue. "Unasema Kiswahili?," I asked. "Do you speak Swahili?"

"Yes," she answered in Swahili. "I understood every word you and your friends spoke and listened silently for I wanted to know if you were hatching an escape."

I told her it would be foolhardy for us to leave for we were in foreign surroundings and it might be worse out there than what we have here. She agreed with our thinking and said it would be a pumbavu (stupid) act. I told her that Kweku and I were trained as trackers and hunters and she answered with a half smile. "You and your friend will go out in the bush tomorrow." Her name was Owusa.

Since this was a warring tribe there were few among them who were qualified hunters so we were welcomed by those who had to provide the meat. They were equipped with metal tipped spears while Kweku and I were given sharp long knives to hack away brush and reeds. The first day out we learned why they were short of meat. They passed over all indications of animal trails and relied mostly on their eyes sighting the animals accidentally.

As we learned to speak Ewe, we showed them that a bent blade of grass or a broken twig was language in the bush. They put Kweku and me in the front and they followed, but there were still mixups when Kweku and I climbed two tall trees to get a good look at some red-fronted gazelle and kept the animals from getting our scent. They thought we were trying to escape. It was more work trying to teach them how to track than it was to snare an antelope.

In time, as we showed them how to trap, snare and corner game, they showed us a little respect for the meat became more plentiful in the village. Kweku and I developed strong upper body and leg muscles by climbing the tall oak trees. This work was a pleasure compared to the back breaking work with the yams and the kola nuts.

This area had a rain forest so the temperature and the humidity were the same as our home village. I missed the oceans and the culture that we were so accustomed to at home. These people were savages, lacked intelligence, discipline and respect for others. A half-civilized tribesman named Kouassi was the only man who treated us as though we were partly human. When I asked him about our fate he said matter-of-factly that when we grew strong we would be sold to Kabes, an infamous slave trader. As I pressed him further he told me how one day we would all be sold; men, women and children to Kabes who would sell us to the Dutch and give Chief Asmak much gold and silver. Then we would be loaded aboard a sailing ship for the west and the crew could pick out the women they wanted for their own use on the voyage. Many seamen had a bad sickness so death would soon take both of them, the woman and the seaman. This news of our future made me sick to my stomach for he also said almost half the slaves reached the western shores dead from disease and starvation.

One cold morning we were sent out in the chilling rain to cut dead firewood. Two young women loaned Kweku and me their shuka (sheet) of kente cloth to cover our heads. We were sent out alone for the other hunters were going out on another hunt. A wily old boar had raided the swine pen and run off with the sows. This boar they called Old Tusk for he was huge and ferocious and defied capture. We set out towards the river where there was an abundance of dead snags and where we had cut wood before.

Having gone only about one-half a mile into the cutting area, Kweku and I stopped short in our tracks for the chimpanzees were stirred up and acting nervous. Normally they would chatter as they gathered up Kola nuts off the ground and then take them up on a limb where they would sit and eat them. Today they were different and we could hear why. Old Tusk was headed in our direction. Kweku scrambled up the only tree that was close by and I was left amid a bunch of stumps. With nowhere to go, I took the shuka off my head and wrapped it around a stump and myself. Tucking the shuka in around my waist, I faced the boar coming at me at full velocity. I raised my ax above my head and waited until he charged into my skirt-covered stump and then I brought my ax down cutting open his skull. He rolled on his side thrashing his feet where he bled to death.

Kweku climbed down from his perch and gave me a hug for he thought he was about to be related to a dead cousin. He congratulated me for my trick move and then proceeded to help me cut vines to wrap around the hind feet and drag the boar back to the village. When we arrived we were greeted with cheers and hand-clapping for we not only stopped a menace but we brought in good meat and valuable giant tusks worth much "fedha." As a reward I was allowed to keep the damaged kente cloth as my own. It was quite a prize for a slave.

■ ■ ■ ■ ■ ■ ■ ■ ■ ■

As the years wore on Kweku and I grew in stature and strength despite regular sadistic beatings ordered by Chief Asmak. He would sit on his porch and have his men line up in two rows so he could only see the two men in the front of each row facing him. Each man had a club about two feet long and by a signal from the chief each row turned so they faced each other. Then two senior women would lead all the male slaves to the end of the row and we were to run as fast as we could up the gauntlet and hope to come out the other end on our feet. We ran right on the heels of the one in front and I could see they all held their hands over their heads to fend off the blows. I hollered to Kweku to try and grab a club out of the hand of one who appeared weaker than ourselves and use it in defense. Some men were tripped and then pummeled while laying helpless on the ground. Some came out the other end bloody and wounded creatures and others lay unconscious.

I got to about the fourth man on my right when I got a good grip on his club and twisted it out of his hand. The man on my left was striking my back but my muscles were tense and hard and the blows did little damage. I ran up the alley of men swinging my club like a madman so I got the most blows on my hands, arms and face. Chief Asmak drowned out all the shrieks and cries with his whooping and laughing. To him the scene was exhilarating and amusing but I saw him as a savage.

Kweku and I were the youngest to suffer but we were chosen because of our height and build. We were fourteen years old but at least six feet tall and as we looked at each other with eyes nearly swollen shut we wondered if the situation could possibly get any worse. Before going to sleep in the evenings, we talked about how we would escape when we got to the new land across the sea for without vision we would die of despair. The thought of revenge also entered into our minds but we didn't know how that could come about as we were always outnumbered.

The only really sensitive and caring person in that whole tribe was a girl our age, the daughter of the slave Owusa who could speak Swahili. After our beating running the gauntlet, she brought us some healing salve made from the African Pepper tree. She would be beaten if she were discovered helping us. Later she came to pick up my prized kente cloth to repair the damage that Old Tusk had done to it. There were tears where the tusks rammed through to the stump. Other than that the cloth was perfect; I would never part with it for it was my only worldly possession.

It would only be by accident that we would run into Poku. She was servant to Chief Asmak's wives so she was restricted to the block house except to fetch food and water and that is how we happened to meet. She had a yoke across her shoulders weighted down by two wooden buckets of water. In our short visit she told us she was surviving but the women would slap her across the face without provocation when she was doing her best to please them. They kept her in the house so she wouldn't be among men and have a baby. They wanted her to take care of their children only. We were satisfied that she was receiving fair care.

Our lives were kept roused by our varied hunting expeditions. The area was blessed with a variety of animals who were leery of humans and difficult to run down. We relied on pits and snares to entrap our prey. On one occasion we snared a well-developed wildebeest and brought him down with spears. While we were cutting him up to carry back to the village, a young hungry lioness with cubs smelled the blood and attacked us. She got the neck of one hunter and wouldn't let go. Since we all had skinning knives in our hands we were momentarily helpless when Kweku jumped on her shoulders and started slashing her throat. He cut a good vein for the blood shot out and splattered all of us. The big cat eventually ran out of strength and rolled on her back thrashing her tail and feet. The hunter was dead, neck broken and head nearly chewed off. When we returned to the village with all the fresh meat, the news of our attack reached the chief's ears and he offered Kweku his freedom to join the tribe. Kweku thanked him but declined his offer.

The meat of the wart hog was considered a delicacy but was the greatest challenge to catch. Kweku and I built a cage with no top or end. It was just the bottom, two sides and one end. We then completed the cage by building the top and end, securing it by two pegs so it operated on a hinge whereby the top and end could be raised and lowered. We drove a sharp peg up through the floor near the front of the box. Then we sharpened two more like pegs to complete the trap. The favorite food of the wart hog was the local nairb root so we stuck this on the end of one of the sharp pegs. With two long poles secured under the trap, eight men carried the cage on their shoulders to an area frequented by the hogs. With the cage secured to a tree so the hog couldn't overturn it, we set about baiting the trap. While Kweku held the lid up, I crawled in and balanced the peg with the nairb root on the tip of the peg protruding from the bottom. Then I took the other peg and steadied it on the bait peg and then to the upraised lid. It took three tries, for the bait peg easily rolled off the tip and from under the upper peg. On the fourth try, the lid stayed upright and I pulled away cautiously from the trap.

In the morning the entire hunting party went running out to the trap to see if it worked. We could hear the hog snorting from a distance. The hog was fighting the cage trying to escape but the cage held. The hunters ran their spears through the cage and into the neck of the fighting hog. The men cheered and slapped us as we carried the carcass back to the village. The tribe was surprised we returned so quickly with the day's supply of meat.

The worst part of being associated with the hunters was that we were also conscripted to go with the raiding party to capture other slaves. They raided the coastal tribes because they were more peaceful and easily subdued. They took Ewe slaves because they spoke the same tongue but the Fante tribe were the best workers so we were raiding their village quite often. Kweku and I put on a sham raid for this was against our way of life but we accompanied them for the alternative was a near death beating.

On the two-day trek back to our village, Kweku and I took the job of herding the women and children for the others treated them so cruelly. We did our best to keep them moving without inflicting more pain on them than they were already feeling. The separating from loved ones was the worst pain of all for we had experienced it first hand.

Kweku and I could not get it straight in our heads why life had to be constant pain and suffering. Why was it necessary for one to enslave another when there was plenty of food and space for every one. What possessed one tribe to enslave another and get so much satisfaction out of seeing others suffer? It was a world we would never understand after living in a peaceful family.

As time passed, Kweku and I grew stronger in mind and body and became as close as any brothers could ever get. We vowed to protect one another and if Poku's life were ever in danger, we would sacrifice our lives to save hers. We sealed this kiapo (oath) by shaking hands in a crisscross fashion as true Bantus.

CAMBRIA TRIBUNE
Friday, October, 27, 1860
THIRD DAY STORY

*I*t was in the year 1807, our seventeenth year, that we were roused out of our kibanda in the wee hours of the morning. All slaves, men and women, were herded in the yard facing the Chief's porch. Our captors were dressed in their hide hoti with painted faces and spears by their sides. They encircled us in a menacing manner chanting and stomping their feet. We knew we were about to have a new experience.

Up on the porch a buxom wife of the Chief brought Poku forward and shoved her out into the crowd. She carried a little bundle in her hand and a look of terror and fright on her face. Kweku and I made our way up to the porch to meet her and keep her close to us for this new happening. The look of fear melted into a beautiful little girl smile for she was a natural beauty endowed with poise and feminine qualities. We hugged as a trio and awaited the Chief to appear.

The bearded, long haired Chieftain came out wearing a colorful leopard skin, a bronze crown and arms and ankles decorated with brass rings. He seated himself and looked us over as though we were loyal subjects. We numbered between thirty to forty humans.

"I am giving you all your freedom," he shouted. "We will journey to the coast at Elmina and there you will be set free to do as you wish. Kiongozi, lead out." We were formed into two columns and ordered to follow Kiongozi at a fast pace. Known trouble-makers were kept in the rear where there were many hate-filled warriors. I recognized these men despite their paint as the savages who beat us as we were forced to run the gauntlet.

We moved at a near trot under the hot morning sun and the humidity caused two sickly women to fall by the wayside. It wasn't until the sun was directly overhead that we stopped for water. The food cart bringing up the rear had a ration for each prisoner, a cut of salt pork and a peck of corn. We received this ration with the warning that it was the last gift to be given us by Asmak so save enough for the rest of the march.

At the last streak of sunset we stopped by the river bend under a large grove of African oaks. We were permitted to go to the river to wash off the day's sweat and dirt and drink until I thought we would split our stomachs. The salt pork gave us an overwhelming thirst. We each pulled up some jackgrass and made us a bedding. I loaned my kente cloth to Poku to lay over the bristly grass. We dozed off listening to the striped hyenas scream to each other.

"Juu, juu" the warrior shouted at daybreak, "up, up." They got great pleasure going about us kicking one and then another. If they were taking us to our freedom why did they act so mean?

We half trotted just as we did the day before except this time we didn't stop when the sun set. We continued on in darkness until we came to the port of Elmina. There we were herded into a dark passageway and then out into a courtyard. They referred to this structure as a castle. Glimmering torches protruding from two sconces cast an eerie light over the seated black bodies huddled in the center of the yard. The painted warriors with their animal hides about themselves looked like moving demons. We were ordered to lay on the ground and not move until morning.

Poku lay next to me gripping my hand as though she were drowning. I comforted her and told her that Kweku and I would let no harm befall her and to find rest so she would be strong for that which lay ahead.

We were awakened by the bright sun and the noise of the city outside the wall. There were more foreign words and strange sounds that were unfamiliar to us. We were allowed to go into a stinking dark room, the vyoo, and then return to the courtyard and eat the remains of our salt pork and corn.

At mid morning the warriors prodded us with their spears and marched us out of the building to the dock at the water's edge. There stood the largest ship with sails that I had ever seen and with white men watching us from the deck. The warriors crowded in behind us and drove us like livestock up the gangplank. Chief Asmak stood behind the warriors with a smile on his bony bearded face. In the wink of an eye, white men with long guns closed in behind the warriors and grabbed their spears. I hollered "Kweku, Kutazama" (look). Some warriors grappled for the long guns but were shot for their efforts. Three shots rang out before the warriors realized they were outnumbered. Then to our surprise, the white men seized Asmak, took off his headgear and his leopard skin coat, confiscated his money pouch and pushed them all up the gangplank behind us.

We were led down a hatchway just as we were on the smaller dhow except this room was much larger and had port holes for light and for air. We slaves were the first to go down so we were directed to the left side. The strange white men with the guns and fully clothed down to their high leather boots pushed us into a cluster, then the painted hide covered captors came down followed by the fighting, raging chief. He was quietly subdued by a blow on the head from the butt end of a gun.

A large bearded white man came down without a gun and stood on the bottom step. He spoke in Ewe, "This is a Dutch ship and we are civilized people. Trouble-makers will be put in irons first. If they continue to be trouble, we will feed them to the sharks. You see this ship is clean. We have washed it down in vinegar, so keep it clean. It is my job to keep you all alive. You will fetch nary a gelding dead. The better you behave the better you will be fed and treated. I will send my sailors down once we get underway to pick a mate for the trip." With that he went up the stairs followed by the men with the guns. The barred hatchcover slammed shut.

An uproar immediately broke out as the women sobbed and the warriors pounced on their chief. It was about to turn into deadly violence when Kweku and I stepped in and defended the chief. We were the tallest and the strongest in the hold and together we would be in charge. I warned the painted savages that now we outnumbered them and Kweku and I would lead the other slaves in combat against them if they did not obey. The memories of the gauntlet were fresh in our minds and it would be difficult to hold the others back who seek retribution.

By the commotion and shouting above, we could detect that the ship was about to get underway. I told Kweku that we must move quickly to save Poku.

We brought the Chief over to the left side of the ship, dragging the whimpering scoundrel by his long hair. Laying his head alongside an eyelet protruding from the deck, I took the attached leg iron and cut off his long hair by severing it between the two irons. Then I did the same with his beard while he cried like a baby pleading for his life.

With the handful of graying long hair, I had Kweku gather pitch from between the bulkhead planks and this we smeared on Poku's head and chin. She was shocked that we would smear the sticky pitch on her but we assured her that we were trying to save her life. We plastered the hair to her head so that it hung down each side and in her face. Then we took the shorter hair and pasted it to her chin. She looked grotesque and repulsive, so then I took my kente cloth and draped it over her head and shoulders. Anyone would take her to be an ugly old man. To finish our drama, we sat her between Kweku and myself and leaned against the bulkhead. We had others sit in front of us so that Poku's feet would not be exposed, then we sat and waited quietly. There was much commotion from the other side for they feared that if the Dutch didn't harm them, we would.

After a short interval, the hatch flew open and a dozen or more dirty scroungy sailors came down the stairs to pick their women. The largest men took the first pick and then the others followed. Two of the sailors chose two young slaves from our side of the ship. None of them gave a second glance to Poku. I doubt they ever thought that she was anything more than a dying old man. Some of the women went willingly thinking it would be a better life than down in the hold but others had to be dragged up the stairs. The hatch slammed shut and there was silence.

Within the hour the hatch opened again and a large metal pot filled with grits was lowered. Then a basket of baked yams came down. This gave us confidence for this was the best food we had had for many days.

When evening came I took Kweku and four others over to the other side and relieved the savages of their hides leaving them in their loin cloths. Those who objected were set upon whereas I had to intervene and come to their rescue. My men were ready to seek revenge but I said it would go hard on them as the Dutch would take them to be violent trouble-makers.

The best two hides went to make a comfortable bed for Poku and we let the others know that she was to be respected as though she were a queen and anyone who questioned it would answer to Kweku and me.

Our next move was to procure a waste barrel for a vyoo so I hollered up through the grating until a sailor appeared. He couldn't understand me so he brought the original huge man who first instructed us in Ewe. I told him that if we were to keep his ship clean, we needed a container. He accepted our request and lowered a barrel with a jug of vinegar for disinfectant. We used the vinegar to cut the pitch out of Poku's hair and off her chin. She was most grateful.

Kweku and I pondered the past and the present. What did they do with Kipawa the crippled boy? We had not seen him at the Asante village for years. We went over to Asmak who lay on the deck in a fetal position and put the question to him. He answered that he had traded him to the Akan tribe to the south for alcohol. We reminded him that he was now being punished for his merciless acts.

In our quiet time before sleep we would dwell on our freedom. We came to the conclusion that we will always be free, it was just our bodies that they can imprison. No one will ever restrain our minds. We will adhere to the principles taught us by our parents.

Our height caught the eyes of the Dutch so as the weeks wore on we were chosen to empty the vyoo barrel, distribute the food and eventually do the heavy work up on deck in the fresh air. We had gained their trust by being quiet and docile and it was obvious that we were from a different tribe. We were more civilized like themselves and could think and act intelligently. We were rewarded with bits of kindness such as bread and oranges and these we shared with Poku.

The one amazing occurrence was to look across the room and look at the painted faces of the former captors. These faces were originally intended to instill fear in us and it really did the opposite. It filled us with anger. I addressed the men on our side and we all agreed that the paint should come off so we took the vinegar over and as an overwhelming group ordered them to use their loincloths and vinegar to wash off the paint. Those who objected were assisted in not too gentle a manner and were sorry that they didn't cooperate on their own. It was humorous to hear these cowards howl when they tried to put their vinegar soaked loincloths back on. They were beginning to understand that we would be in charge for the remainder of the voyage.

In our close contact with the crew, we learned why we were not mistreated. It seems that on previous voyages the hold would be so tightly packed with slaves that they would lose almost half of them from disease, insanity and all forms of mistreatment, especially malnutrition. As the dead would be thrown overboard, the Captain could see his profits dwindling so a new approach was adopted. Providing more clean space, more food and no mistreatment meant higher profits. So we who were transported later were the more fortunate. We had no deaths whatsoever.

Poku, Kweku and I decided to keep practicing our mother tongue and use it as a means to communicate in privacy. Swahili would be like a secret code for us.

CAMBRIA TRIBUNE
Tuesday, October 31, 1860
FOURTH DAY STORY

*A*fter three months at sea, we approached land. A new land that I could not imagine. The weather was unfavorable; scudding clouds overhead and a strong easterly wind convinced the captain to drop anchor offshore and wait out the weather.

Looking back, I can say that those three months were the best we had since we were kidnapped from our home village. We were not mistreated and once the crew discovered how helpful Kweku and I were to them, we received better food which we shared with Poku. At the end of a hard day on deck, holy stoning (using pumice on) the foredeck on our hands and knees, we would take our ration of meat and bread down to share it with Poku. She would greet us with a broad smile showing perfect milk-white teeth; she was beautiful.

In the morning we had a light fog that hung about twenty foot above the water and the Captain ordered the anchor weighed so we could proceed. Kweku and I were called up on deck to help turn the capstan and then stow the anchor chain. After the work was done, we were allowed to stay in the bow and watch our approach into Charleston, threading our way between the islands into Charleston harbor. We tied up to the dock that held the longest building I had ever seen. Such a massive structure boggled my mind, there were no buildings like that in Elmina.

Many white men came aboard in fancy dress and hats. They were interested in the ship's cargo. It was then that I discovered that in the forward hold were hides of leather and ivory tusks.

Kweku and I were ordered to bring the slaves out on deck by two's washing them down with water from the harbor using soapwort roots to scrub them clean. Then they shackled the left leg of one to the right leg of the other. The women were led off unrestrained. We hollered to Poku, "Hapana jambo" (don't worry). We were led into the long warehouse on the dock and to our surprise there were other slaves there who had just been unloaded from an English ship. These people were half-starved, dirty and even had children in their group. When I could get close enough to them I asked them in Ewe and Swahili where they were from. Once he understood my question, he answered "Senegambia." That was foreign to me but I knew he was from Africa.

Our group was led into a small anteroom with tables and benches and metal plates were set on the table. We were given a large portion of grits and pork belly; a bucket of water and a dipper was placed on each table. Whatever our fate, the Dutch wanted us to appear healthy.

In the background our Dutch captors were engaged in an argument with other well dressed, hatted white men. It appeared that the discussion entailed the sale of us all in one transaction or none at all. It seemed to be the opinion of the dealers that slaves from our area were the most desired in South Carolina. Finally a truce was reached and the lusty arguing subsided. One white man with top hat and a long-tailed coat agreed to buy twenty of us. He went about picking the healthiest and strongest of the lot. We who were of lighter skin were chosen for we stood taller above the rest. We were unshackled from our partners and led to the outside.

An impression that is deeply imprinted on my mind is the open slave market outside the long building. On one stage were naked men and women and on another the men were dressed in white man's clothes complete with shoes, coat and hat. Some faces expressed appalling fear and others looked like standing dead. This was a land of terrible people.

The buyer of our lot was known as a broker. He represented various plantation owners who paid him to purchase field and house slaves for them. Our broker was named Master Paisley. He was cunning and without conscience or feeling.

We were all led aboard a small riverboat and guarded by two armed men and Kweku and I were amazed how many people only one armed man could control.

Our small boat sailed out into the open harbor and headed in a northwesterly direction up the Cooper River. It was full of turns and bends but after a short time the river straightened out into a wide sweep of fresh clear running water.

Our boat pulled onto the left shore alongside a small wooden dock. The large sign overhead read "Mepkin Plantation." The two armed men jumped ashore first and then Master Paisley. The first man he pointed to with his swagger stick was Kweku since he was so tall and outstanding. Then he took seven others. As Kweku was directed to leave, I grabbed his hand and said "Kwa heri, rafiki, Tutaonana baadaye" (Good-bye friend, see you later). Poku just spoke softly "Kweku!"

I was to be delivered elsewhere. Master Paisley aimed to get the most for his cargo by splitting us up. We were held at bay by an armed man on the dock while Paisley and another armed man led the others off. It was then that I noticed Paisley had a hand gun beneath his coat. After what appeared to be a long wait for us on the small boat, the two captors returned and the boat was shoved off and we were on our way downstream to Charleston.

Leaving my cousin behind was a heart wrenching ordeal. Kweku is a very stoic person and the only emotion he ever really showed was anger but as he walked away on the deck, he turned and with raised fist in a firm voice said "Uhuru" (Freedom). He remembered our conversation on our first night aboard the Dutch ship. This country would make us free men!

On our way downstream, I cradled Poku in my arms. She looked up at me with her sparkling brown eyes and asked, "Are we ever going to see Kweku again and are we ever going to be free?" I assured her that the time would come when we would once again be together living as free people in this spacious land.

We put in at Charleston at the same dock we had left. Paisley's home was located in that town so he had his men put us back in the holding room we had occupied the night before.

The autumn nights were quite cold on the waterfront so I bundled Poku in my kente cloth and held her tight against me so we could share body heat. The dock was stacked with cotton bales and I hoped that we would be able to gather enough scraps to make a little bedding but we were not afforded that luxury.

We were awakened in the morning by an amplified voice shouting prices. Looking out through the boards of the building I could see a man with a cone shaped horn asking bids for slaves in ragged shirts and pants. These were apparently resold slaves who were either lazy, sickly or trouble-makers and the owners were asking an offer. This area was a human stockyard!

The two guards with guns came in to see that we all went to the vyoo and then they brought us a bushel basket of wild grapes, hominy and chitlings in a large bucket. Poku and I were disliked by the others because we were different, of lighter skin. Had I not been bigger than they, we would not have gotten any of the food.

Mr. Paisley came in and motioned for me to follow him. I took Poku's hand and began to follow. He signaled that I come alone but I let him know that I would not leave Poku with those evil creatures. He wanted to know if she was my wife and I nodded no and wrapped my arms about her. Poku said "Angu Kinga" which means "my protector." He relented and let us follow him. He took me to a post with numbers and had me stand against it. "Six feet, seven inches" he laughed. This niggard will bring me a bonus."

We were reloaded aboard Paisley's boat for the next leg of our journey and immediately a fight broke out among the others as to where they would sit. The guards just stood by and watched for they didn't want to deliver slaves who were bruised and cut. That would mean they were trouble-makers. I waded in between them and cuffed them on their ears. They got the message and quieted down.

The boat took a northeasterly course along the coast, weaving between the islands and staying clear of the open sea that appeared a bit choppy. We put in at Georgetown but were kept on board and guarded by two more armed men who took a fancy to Poku. As they came over and grabbed her arm, I pushed the both of them to the deck. Before they could get to their feet, our other guards came to my rescue and warned them not to touch any of us as long as we did not try to escape.

At the break of day, we got underway and sailed up the Waccamaw River until it narrowed down to a stream so small that our boat grounded. Paisley had us transfer to a large wagon with high boarded sides pulled by a team of black mules.

Looking at the faces of the others as we jostled along I could see anticipation and anxiety for we were all apprehensive as to the treatment we would receive at our final destination.

Stories ran a course from a leisurely job of watching cattle to a backbreaking job of working fourteen hours a day, seven days a week in the cotton fields. The two new slaves that were added to our group in Georgetown showed us their arms that were eaten almost to the bone by tapping pine trees for resin to make turpentine. They looked like lepers I had seen at Elmina.

Our wagon pulled up at a pair of large iron gates on the evening of the second day of arduous traveling. We spent much time driving along swamplands that over-produced their fair share of mosquitoes. It would be a relief to get into a building where we would be sheltered from these biting insects.

We were unloaded under the watchful eyes of the four guards into four small cabins. Poku was placed in a cabin where women stood outside gaping at the new load of black humanity. As Poku was led silently away I shouted "'Tutaonana baadaye" (See you later") trying to assure her that I would be close by.

Our cabin held four bunks and just enough room in the middle for two people to pass. It was mere shelter. I asked the others to be quiet and quit their senseless chatter for we would need the rest for what lay ahead. I fell into a deep restful sleep.

The sun had not yet broken over the horizon when we heard a knocking on our door and then the next and on down the row of shanties, the knocking faded away. We roused out of our beds and stepped out into the pine woods to relieve ourselves. There was one bucket of water and a wash basin and towel for the four of us to clean ourselves the best we could. Having been raised by the water, we were taught to bathe daily so this life was foreign to me.

The food was brought to us by an old white haired slave with a two wheel cart. He had warm hominy and chitlings and a fresh bucket of water accompanied by a warm smile and words of reassurance that "God will be with us this day." I had no idea what he meant but it sounded good to me.

After eating, we, the new arrivals, were marched up before the manor house and placed in position for inspection by our new overseers. I gave Poku a warm embrace and held her to my side.

After what seemed to be eternity, a well dressed red-headed man with an extended forehead and heavy mustache came out through the huge double doors, followed by a retinue of black men and women. He hesitated on the porch for a moment staring blankly at us and then proceeded down the steps to get a closer look.

He stopped first in front of Poku and then snapped his fingers and said "Lizzie." Immediately a large black woman in black dress, white cap and apron took Poku by the hand and led her into the house. Next he eyed me from head to toe and looking up into my face he spoke to a black elderly man who came over and opened my mouth and pulled my lips back. The white man wanted to see my teeth, to me that was a very odd gesture. The red-headed man then touched the elderly man with his swagger stick and he released my lips and jaw. The master smiled at me with a smirk of satisfaction and passed on down the line to examine the others. Then we were dismissed to go back and stand before our cabins.

After a brief wait the master, a young man my age, and four muscular black men rode up on horseback. The four blacks dismounted and stood at attention beside the young man's horse. The master spoke, "My name is Master Buford Jowers and this is my son Ashley. He will be in charge and will represent me and anyone who does not show him proper respect, disrespects me. Insubordination will be dealt with by these four faithful servants who know how to break a renegade and bring him to his knees so I would advise you all to walk the line and obey.

"Ashley, I want you to learn how powerful brain is over brawn and this tall niggard here is your testing ground. He will bend to your every whim and desire or else feel the leather across his back. You! What is your name?"

I answered "Kaka Zuri" and with that I received a cut across my face by a set of reins delivered by one of the blacks.

"Kaka Zuri, Master, you answer" the servant barked.

"Kaka Zuri, Master" I repeated.

"You see Ashley, my boy, this niggard is so stupid he has the brain of a child. I'll leave it up to you to educate him."

The young red-headed man was about my age and I was eighteen that fall. He had thin bony features with flared nostrils and paper thin lips. He reeked of evil.

He looked down at me from his horse and in a scornful way said, "From now on your name will be Dolt. Dolt Jowers. Now you boys take him over to the branding shed and then out in the fields where he can earn his keep."

As I was being marched between the four mounted blacks, I thought to myself, "If that stunted malcontent can't understand that I come from a different country and can hardly comprehend what he is saying, then it is he and not I who should receive the degrading appellation. "

At a blacksmith shed two of the men dismounted and took hold of each of my arms. Then the other two dismounted and before I was aware of their mission, my side guards tripped me and the man behind jumped on my back. I was pinned to the ground. Before I could struggle, a searing hot iron burned into my right shoulder. My body stiffened in a reflex action but the mission was complete. I had been branded with the letters B.J. Buford Jowers had his mark on my body but my soul and mind were still free. I also realized that there was a bitter prejudice against me because of my lighter skin. The other blacks resented me. I was not accepted!

CAMBRIA TRIBUNE
Monday, November 6, 1860
FIFTH DAY STORY

*T*he main crops on the Jowers plantation were cotton and tobacco. The cotton had been harvested and now the tobacco leaves were turning a golden brown and needed to be cut and hauled to the drying sheds. Because of my height, I picked the bundles of cut and bound tobacco and loaded them onto a wagon that moved slowly through the field. Two hands worked the right side while I had to keep up on the left as the wagon wouldn't stop to compensate for the double duty I was assigned. I adjusted to the rhythm and moved at a slow trot. The only reprieve I got was when the wagon got filled and the two slaves on the other side had to stop the wagon to throw the bundles on the high stack which I reached with no difficulty.

Upon reaching the drying shed, we climbed to the highest peak of the building and with others handing the bundles up to us, we hung the tobacco in neat rows so it got air from all sides. When our wagon was empty we returned for a new load. The only comfort to the job was to see Poku coming with a bucket of water and a dipper to quench our thirst.

"My kinga," she said her face lighting up. "It is so good to see you. Are you being treated properly?"

I answered that all was well with me. How was she fairing?

She answered that she was working the massive house with other women who were of diverse temperament but

44

the food, clean clothes and bed made up for the mistreatment. I reassured her that I would not leave without her and that I felt a great love for her. That was the first time I ever mentioned love for she was sixteen at that time and had matured nicely.

The work never came to an end. We worked outside at every opportunity and when it was too wet we worked in the shed. The Jowerses bought the new gin machines so that cotton was cleaned right there on the plantation. The other farms in the area were shipping their cotton to England to be cleaned and made into cloth.

As I was learning the language, I was also interested in learning my letters so that I could read like the white folks. My first letters were "York, Penna" which had been etched on the machinery. I memorized those letters and would write them on the dirt with a stick. Someday I'd learn all the letters!

Master Ashley never missed an opportunity to harass me no matter how hard I worked and tried to please him. He would approach me on horseback while I labored in the field and would question me in such a way that if I said "No Master" I would get hit or if I said "Yes Master" I would take the same punishment. He always had at least one of the four lackeys with him and they carried a long whip with a leather covered metal handle. Master Ashley beat me to show his superiority but the lackeys beat me to impress their master and stay in good standing so as to receive special favors.

The hardest work started in the Spring when the fields were prepared for the cotton crop. When the furrows were opened, I would follow behind a wagon loaded with sacks of feed and drop off sacks in each row at designated intervals. Then each of us would load a sack on our back and drop seeds from each hand into the furrows. It was back breaking work to the point that some would eventually drop to their knees when their backs gave out. The lackeys on horseback kept an eye out for stragglers; if they were feigning they were whipped, but if they were truly hurt they were given a hoe and made to pull the dirt over the seeded furrows.

Poku with her bucket and dipper was a welcome and refreshing sight. She carried a wooden yoke across her shoulders so she could haul two buckets at once. She would walk many miles in a day but never complained because it brought smiles from the field hands.

In the heat of the humid summer South Carolina sun, we all had to chop cotton from the first break of daylight till the last rays of light. We were fed salty pork and given lots of water. Poku came down the rows with a mule drawn cart just wide enough to get between the rows. She had wooden blocks floating on the surface of each tub of water to keep it from splashing; a trick she had learned from her mother. She whispered to me that Ashley was always watching her when he was in the house. This made her feel very uneasy. I told her that when the tobacco got high in the late summer, we would plan an escape to the north where they had no slaves.

Every evening when the others talked, I kept both ears open to learn what they had discovered in this new land. Some had been to other parts of the state and they would talk about the land, the swamps and the dangers.

If I learned a few new letters a month, I felt very proud and pleased. Numbers also fascinated me. They had a rhythm about them that brought about a harmony. I thought how wonderful they work out! They come alive!

■ ■ ■ ■ ■ ■ ■ ■ ■ ■

By late August the crop of Bright tobacco was well along and the chances of sneaking off the plantation by disappearing down the long rows was quite possible. I told Poku that our escape to the north was about to take place and she should plan what clothes and articles she will want to make up a bindle.

It was on a night of a full moon that I silently made my way to the stables to steal a hoof trimming knife I needed to take along on our escape north. As I crawled to a side door I could hear voices within. A house boy was talking to a stable boy describing the death of a house servant. As I listened there was no mistake that they were describing Poku. I jumped to my feet and bolted into the room nearly upsetting their lantern. I grabbed both of them by the front of their shirts and asked them what happened to Poku. The house boy shook and looked at me wild-eyed as he said he heard she died but he had doubts about the whole affair. Pressing him further, he admitted that he surmised Master Ashley killed her for he had mistreated other women in his bedroom. I shook him harder trying to squeeze every bit of information out of him. He explained that Ashley would ask the cook to send a maid to his room with food. Each time the maid returned in a sullen, disheveled, upset mood. When he specifically asked for Poku, the cook would make an excuse that she was busy with another task. Today Ashley managed to have someone send Poku up to his room with his meal. The next news we heard was that she died. That is all he really knew.

I turned and walked away, thanking the two for their help. First I lost Kweku, my life long friend and now my beloved Poku who I promised to protect. "Kinga" she called me. Her protector. I felt a total failure and thought the least I could do was to lose my life in killing the miserable Ashley.

When I returned to my cabin, the others there asked me what I was crying about. I related what was disclosed to me and my intention of killing Ashley. They said I would be killed by his guards before I could get near him so to abandon the idea before losing my own life needlessly.

Sleep was replaced by a phantasm of nightmares, more like a stupor. I rolled and tossed until the knock came to the door and the message that we would bury a house slave before going out into the field. Was it out of respect that we were afforded this privilege or was it out of guilt? I would not pass up this one last chance to say "Kwa heri" (Good bye).

We all stood on either side of the back door as a house servant came out carrying a crude pine box followed by an elderly servant carrying the other end. I pushed them aside and took his place at the foot of Poku's coffin. We slowly marched to the slave cemetery while all the others sang a dirge about a "Sweet chariot that would carry Poku home." The tears streamed down my face soaking the front of my tattered blouse. When we reached a newly dug grave only a few feet deep, we sat the box down. Before anyone could intervene, I opened the box to see my beloved baby in her servant dress, her eyes swollen and her lips and face so badly bruised that only I would know that it was my Poku. Somebody pulled me away, but I stole one last glance at my life long friend as the rising sun cast its morning rays across the cloudless sky. No birds sang on the plantation that day.

I went out into the fields to cut the last of the tobacco but my heart was not there. I was totally irrational for my mind raced from one extreme to another. I finally was conscious of the deep love that I had for Poku. It was hidden in the deep recesses of my heart and I never let it come to the surface. Then I thought of myself as the only one to avenge her death for after all I had been her sole protector since she was eight years old. I felt somewhat responsible.

As the sun set and the day came to an end, I made preparation to leave the Jowers plantation. All I could see in my mind was the slave cemetery with a single slat of wood for a head stone. I didn't want to come to the same end as those poor souls.

Using the blanket from my bed as a sack, I packed my kente cloth, a bottle for water, a sack of grain and a head of cabbage I had stolen from the food cellar as well as a hoof knife from the stable. With this bindle strapped across my shoulder, I lit out across the tobacco field in an easterly direction. Had I not been so distraught, I would have been more organized and prepared for my long trip to the north and to freedom.

After trudging all night in the dark and evading night riders by lying in the ditch when I heard them approach, I was ready to collapse at the first sight of light of the new day. My training as a hunter helped me to think like an animal and find a place where no human would discover me. I found such a place in high grass beneath a cedar tree where a deer had bedded down. Using my bindle for a pillow, I closed my eyes and slept till the sun was descending in the sky.

The grain and the cabbage tasted mighty good to me and then I thought that this would be a good time to climb the cedar and look over the countryside. The first object to catch my eye was a field of red and yellow tomatoes off to my left. It wasn't too far off the road so I figured that would be my first move after dark, to steal a sack of ripe tomatoes.

By now I knew the Jowerses would know I was missing so I planned my route from the tomato patch to the Little Pee Dee River where I could hide my scent from the Jowerses' dogs. They would have a good smell of me from my sweat stained straw mattress.

It was by accident that I found a creek only a few feet wide flowing in my direction so I waded all night to the north. At daybreak I found a tree growing along the stream with roots exposed out into the water. So as not to touch ground and leave a scent I climbed the tree and found a crotch high enough to lay down on and give me a good view of all activity below. Knowing how the large monkeys back in Bidiana built a nest in a crotch, I took my bindle and used it as a sling between the two limbs running from the crotch. This gave me enough area to stretch out and yet keep me safe from falling when I dozed off. I just had to remember not to roll in my sleep.

The yelping of hounds brought me out of a sound slumber and I figured there were from four to five dogs. They became more distant as the afternoon wore on; they were following downstream, as I thought they would, trying to find my scent on the shore. I struck out while it was still light but kept a low profile. It was dark when I approached the Little Pee Dee and immediately searched the banks for two logs that would hold me afloat. I wasted an hour finding the right debris and lashing them together with my bindle cord.

With my body laying prostrate between the two logs, I had a good stable means of paddling myself down the river and heading for the opposite bank. My followers must have stopped for the night for I could not hear their dogs in the clear night air, only an owl and a whippoorwill calling to their mates. By daybreak, I put ashore and found a safe place near a corn field to bed down. The corn had been harvested and the stalks had been shucked so I took an armful from one shock and made myself a comfortable bed in the high brush. The freedom was exhilarating and sleep came easily.

When I awoke I could hear cows and a barking dog so I climbed a pine tree to reconnoiter. There was a small farm off in the distance and between the farm and the cornfield lay an orchard and I could discern red apples.

As darkness settled in I crept up through the corn field using the high corn shucks to hide behind; I didn't want to attract that dog. As I neared the orchard I got on my belly and silently approached the apple tree like a hungry lion. The fallen apples were good enough for me; I didn't want to risk standing up for I might be seen by someone sitting on the porch. I grabbed about a dozen solid orange sided apples and putting them in my bindle, I sneaked back to the river bank.

I found myself eventually getting on softer ground as I headed north. The brush turned into tubes so I knew it was a swampy area. The going got harder as the cushy ground got wetter and I found myself in water up to my knees. Hoping to eventually get onto solid ground I veered off to the left heading a little northwest. Without a bit of warning I felt a sharp pain below my right knee. I had been bitten by a cottonmouth water moccasin. This, I thought, would be a terrible place to die. The poison moves very fast as I had to work in the dark and suck the venom out.

I found a little mound of dry ground where a tree had rotted and built a little soil. Taking the hoof knife, I cut where I felt the fang marks and in a double up position I managed to suck furiously at the bleeding cut. Being seven feet tall, I figured I had a better chance than a small person but I was beginning to feel woozy. I struggled to my feet and headed north to the best of my ability. In my mind I had to tell somebody that Poku did not die. She was killed by Ashley Jowers.

CAMBRIA TRIBUNE
Wednesday, November 15, 1860
SIXTH DAY STORY

As I passed from a dream into reality, I realized that I was laying on a wooden floor in a strange cabin. A bearded rugged white man was staring into my face.

"Can you hear me?" he asked. I shook my head yes.

"We found you draped over a snag and thought you were dead. Since you were warm we brought you home and discovered your swollen knee. We recognized the snake bite so we're treating it the best we know how. We usually save half of the victims but you did a good job of slowing the venom in your blood. We'll doctor you until you can travel and then you'll have to move on for we see Jowerses' mark on your back."

I asked them where I was and who were they.

"You are on Snow Island and my name is Tom Marion, son of Francis Marion. You probably never heard about my Daddy, but he bushwhacked the British from this here island in the last war. A remnant of his band just stayed on here in the swamp because we like the freedom and privacy from all outsiders. You are too long for our bunks so we made you comfortable here on the floor. You'll be fit to move on in a few days. My wife will feed you well and get you back on your feet."

"I'll be forever beholding to you" I told them. "I'm just trying to get north and live as a free man."

He told me that he didn't cotton to slavery and wanted no part of it but he didn't want to get involved in the underground movement of helping runaways. I told him I understood and would take off as soon as possible.

They restored my faith in humanity. I found white people who acted decent and whom I could trust. They gave me help in understanding survival in the swamp and how to find the best route north. Their food was the best I had ever eaten in my whole life. Those people knew how to live off the land.

On the fourth day of my stay on Snow Island, Mr. Marion fixed me up with a rawhide rucksack full of dry jerky, my bottle filled with a rich broth soup and dried fruits enough to last me a week. Mr. Marion had two of his friends take me by their flat bottom boat out through a cleared waterway to the edge of the swamp. There the solid earth met the swamp area and a path was cleared through the brush that led to a roadway going into the little town of Brandon.

The swamp men put me ashore and gave me a departing gift of a roasted deer shank. They told me to eat it before I ate my jerky as it would spoil within a few days. They showed me the route to take north, and warned me to keep low during daylight hours for "darkies" were always suspect.

Thanking my benefactors I headed out toward the road all the while looking for a place to hole up until dark. I also discovered that my leg had a ways more to go before I could walk normally. The pain was bearable because the purpose was freedom.

The deer meat was lean and tasty and would give me strength to walk the long night. I struck out at nightfall on the road to Brandon but as I neared the town I took a route out across the field to circumvent the town. I passed from one field to another, climbing fences and going over hedgerows. At day break I found a farm that had been abandoned years ago and was in a dilapidated state. As I entered the farm house my foot went through the floor so I backed out and headed for the barn. There were a few bats and barn swallows flying about in the loft, so I figured I could live with that. I bunched up what straw was on the barn floor and took it to the loft for bedding. I felt safe enough to fall into a deep sleep.

When I awoke I feasted on Mrs. Marion's broth and the deer meat. I thought that when I got north and get settled down I'm going to eat victuals like this every day. I had enough deer meat left for another meal and I also noticed another dividend. My leg felt less painful and some of the swelling had gone down. My stomach was full and my spirits high so I set out again for the north.

I figured that by now I must be in North Carolina for I had traveled quite a distance. Climbing over a rail fence I came across a wide well-used road that seemed to be a main highway. There was a road sign that read "Lumberton 50 miles." That meant that this road led to a big town so I took a route parallel to the road so as not to be surprised by any night travelers.

Walking beneath a clear star studded sky gave me an invigorating feeling so I sang to myself the song I heard about the "Sweet Chariots." Looking up it appeared that the pine trees had the stars hanging from their branches but then my reverie was disturbed by the sound of animals coming up behind me. When I could make out the rushing figures as a pack of wild dogs, I took to the nearest tree like a frightened monkey. Then the dogs started barking savagely and I feared that they would draw attention to my presence.

My scamper up the tree reminded me of Kweku and the time Old Tusk came after us. It is amazing how fast you can climb when your life is in danger. After catching my breath I then thought out a solution to my predicament. I took out the shank bone and gave the dogs a smell of the tasty meat. Before I parted with it, I devoured the lean meat myself and left the fat and bone for the half-starved dogs. With all the strength I could muster from my perch, I threw the bone back down the path I had just walked. The dogs rushed in a tight pack down the trail to the bone and there was the doggonest awfulest dog fight I ever saw. While they were occupied I jumped to the ground and ran like a gazelle to the north.

Daybreak found me on the west side of town in a dense grove of longleaf pines. I noticed how they differed from the slash pines we had on the Jowers plantation. This thick stand of pines would be a good place to rest for the day.

Lumberton was a bustling town for I could hear a steam driven saw mill working all day disturbing my sleep. I had never had to sleep near so much noise in all my life but I figured I had better get used to the white man's world.

When I became fully awake, I appeased my hunger pangs with the last of the soup, a little jerky and some dried apples. The foreboding storm told me that this was going to be a miserable night for walking. The inability to see a good distance left a good chance of walking into danger so I looked for shelter.

Crawling through a boarded fence I found myself on a large plantation, probably the owner of the sawmill for who else could afford lumber for such a fence. As I made my way through an orchard I came upon a well with the overhead shelter and windlass. I lowered the bucket and heard it hit water a short distance down. In a few minutes I rewound the windlass and pulled in a bucket of fresh cool water. As I was drinking from a bucket I sensed that I was being watched. From out behind a large apple tree stepped a skinny black who really startled me. A wind was beginning to whip up so I thought that was why I didn't hear him approach. He asked me what I was doing there and I told him that I was heading North. He asked if I was free or a runaway and I told him the truth. He asked me if I wanted company and I agreed to take him along but first he wanted to go back to his cabin and fix a bindle. I agreed to accompany him and he took me to a two man cabin the size of a large dog house. There was a lamp lighted inside and another gray haired slave sitting on his bunk. I introduced myself and the man who brought me in said his name was Toka and would I wait until he got his shirt off the clothesline. He closed the door and I could hear the bolt slide into place from the outside. I felt very uneasy and gave thought to rushing the door with all my weight but maybe this man was truthful. When a few minutes passed I knew I was in trouble and slammed my body against the door with all my strength. I landed outside on the ground on top of the door. I started running as fast as I could away from all structures to get myself off that plantation. The sound of horses hooves told me that I was being run down and that I didn't have much of a chance for escape.

One horse came up on my left and the other on my right and they slipped a rope over my shoulders and around my arms. As they galloped away the rope tightened around me and dragged me to the ground. I was dragged to what must have been built as a holding cell for I was thrown in and my bindle stripped from me. That was the first time I was without my kente cloth so I knew it meant bad luck. A steel grate slammed shut in the darkness and I could hear the snap of a lock.

My first impulse was to shake the door for weakness. Then I went to the other three walls but they were heavily reinforced. Then I tried lifting the roof but it showed no sign of movement. I laid down on the dirt floor and pondered my fate.

What right do people have over the lives of others? Are most people in this world evil, both black and white? Must I live a slave until I die, enduring punishment just for the sake of amusement for others? Why does the color of my skin prevent me from having a wife and family like the white man? Maybe Poku is better off than I am and it would be better if I joined her in death. The problem is that right now I don't have a choice for there is no way that I can kill myself in here.

I passed out from sheer exhaustion and was awakened by the rattling of the cell door. I looked up and there were four black faces looking in on me as though I were a caged animal. One of the men was the skinny old fellow who met me at the well and locked me in his cabin. I rose to my feet and approached the door. Towering over all four of them I made a grab for the man named Toka but he jumped back.

"You are an evil man," I told him. "You are a liar and may your fate be a deserving one," I said angrily.

Someone came with a key and opened the door. There stood two white men with drawn pistols. They ordered me to the ground and then had the other men rip off my shirt. They saw the brand on my back and compared it to a book that they searched through.

"The Jowers brand," one of them shouted. "We'll find out what reward is offered."

I was ordered up off the wet ground and back into my cell. Later the two men returned and put iron shackles on my ankles. I felt totally defeated. What chance does a slave have in this world to live as a free animal. I will have to bide my time for I am still young.

A stout woman slave in black dress and white apron with a scowl on her face handed me a small bucket of gruel and some sow belly through the grate. Without a word she stomped off.

The food was unbearable after eating with the Marions on Snow Island. It was like the swill that they served to their swine.

A stocky black man with a rifle strapped to his back came and unlocked my cage. He had me hobble to a long pole in the yard where I could see hoof prints had made a large round path the length of the pole. He first chained my wrists to a ring on the pole and then he unshackled my feet. He ordered me to push on the pole that in turn rolled a heavy weight over the cotton seeds. This in turn produced cotton seed oil. I evidently replaced an ox or a mule. Had my mother or father seen me in this position I would have died of shame.

No one had to tell me what would happen if I refused or if I slowed down. There were always ever present lackey slaves with long horse whips just too eager to use them. They often went about snapping them in the air or cutting leaves off a limb with one slash.

At night when I was released from the push pole and returned to my cell shackled, I found my blanket and kente cloth on the ground. My jerky and dried fruit and knife were missing.

I dug a hole in the corner for vyoo and used the dirt to cover up after I used it. The air coming in through the grated door helped to keep the air clean but the nights were getting very cold. I asked the old woman who brought my food to please bring me some covering but she walked away ignoring my plea.

My only reprieve from the push pole came with the rain. The oil was to be kept pure so they didn't grind during the downpours. That all came to a change when they built a carrousel roof over the operation so I could continue in all kinds of weather.

The slave feeding the seed to the grindstone was moved by my pathetic task and took me into his confidence. He told me that word was sent to my owners asking the amount of the reward in case they found me. In the meantime they were in no hurry to collect the money as long as I stayed productive. Also he mentioned that the other workers believed that I was a white mixture because of my lighter color and Caucasian features so they shunned me. I answered that I was from the Bantu tribe who had mixed with the Arabs but that did not satisfy them.

A dirty worn out patch quilt was stuffed in the metal door when I returned at dark. It was a gift I will not forget. The penetrating bone chilling cold would cause me to shake from within so I lost much sleep just trying to keep my body heat. The quilt had been made of layers of material and had much weight. I rolled up in my blanket and then the quilt and felt the first warmth in my cell since I was locked up.

There had been some negotiations going on for the feed man said he heard I was about to be returned. It was the last of the year and a light snow powdered the ground when a team pulled up in the yard drawing a screened sided wagon with the bright green letters across the side, "High Sheriff of Florence County." Then I knew for certain that I was being returned to face Master Ashley. If I could meet him one on one, even though he had his whip, I could end his life and settle the bad blood that was between us.

When the Sheriff saw my size he asked for back up while loading me in his wagon. There he shackled my feet and my wrists with a chain going from my wrists down to my ankles. I must have appeared to be a great threat to him even though I showed no resistance. I accepted it with the thought that if I get the chance I'll run away until I eventually live as a free man.

CAMBRIA TRIBUNE
Saturday, November 25, 1860
SEVENTH DAY STORY

The driver of the jail wagon was a deputy who was in no hurry to get back to his district. We ambled along the country roads and I could watch out through the screened sides to get the lay of the land in daylight. I took mental notes for I would be coming this way again some day bypassing the swamp.

Although the deputy sat only a few feet from me on the other side of a protective screen, he never spoke to me, only to the team. I played a game in my mind searching for a safe route from the highway and safe places to hold up in my make believe escape going in the opposite direction.

The wagon served as my holding cell for the two days it took us to reach Florence County. We first stopped off at the Sheriff's office in town where the deputy was relieved and a new deputy and the High Sheriff himself took over the team. The Sheriff was struck by my size for I nearly touched the roof from a sitting position. I would like to have read his mind.

We arrived back at Jowers plantation a little after noon and I was left sitting in the wagon. Soon the four lackeys came out and peered into the wagon. They laughed and teased me by telling of the reward I was about to receive for coming back to visit them. In my best language I told them how Msaliti (traitors) were rewarded by my Bantu people for it was considered the worst crime anyone could commit.

Master Ashley rode up on his mare to oversee my return. I was pulled out of the wagon and both wrist and ankle restraints were removed. Master Ashley, with his lips stretched tight and his nostrils flared, shouted in a loud falsetto voice, "Boy, I'm going to teach you a lesson you'll never forget. I'm your Master and you're my servant and you never leave without my permission."

In a blind rage with the image of Poku in her coffin, I grabbed Ashley by the thigh and lifted him from the saddle and threw him to the ground. The lackeys and the Sheriffs started beating me with their metal handled whips and I don't know if I was able to stomp the red-headed serpent or not for the last I remember was seeing this snake on the ground and feeling stunning blows to my head.

Here, at this moment, my new life began. Many of your readers may not believe this but I have no reason to lie. This is what I experienced and I hope you can understand.

I approached a bright light. It got brighter the nearer I got until it was stronger than the sun except that I could look directly into it. Then a blue glow grew out of the light and there in all her glory stood Poku in a heavenly blue gown. The moisture in her eyes sparkled like miniature stars. She spread her arms open as to receive me and spoke, "My kinga. Now it is my turn to protect you. You will continue to have hardships but you will understand they are necessary."

My complete self was overwhelmed. I wanted to remain in that surrounding the rest of my life. Then a very tall figure appeared standing behind Poku and I immediately recognized my father. He had a faint smile and as though he could read my mind, he shook his head no. There was a sort of barrier between us, a film, for they were behind a kind of opaque glass. Then Poku spoke.

"Your new master needs you to complete your task. You must return but I will be always with you. When you hear the word *saba* (*seven*) you'll know that I am with you. Tutaonana baadaye! (See you later)."

I quickly called "What is my new master's name?" She said "Love."

The first sounds I heard was a deep male voice saying, "I think he's going to make it" and then a woman's voice saying "Thank God." Then I went off into a deep silent sleep again.

The warm spoon of soup touching my lips brought me back to a conscious state and I could feel a hand beneath my head. I opened my eyes and found myself looking into a bright shiny plump ebony face.

"It's alright baby," she said. "Take some of this warm soup to help you regain your strength."

"I thought I heard a man's voice," I asked.

"Oh that was Dr. Bill. I had him come over to check you out to see if you had a chance to live again. Those animals beat you to where you were more dead than alive. I waded into them with a corn broom and beat on them until they backed off. They were beating your lifeless body and laughing as Master Ashley egged them on. I had the house servants move you here to my cabin."

"Who are you?," I asked.

"My name is Aunt Mae. Mae Bell. I'll take care of you and get you on your feet. The doctor said you have a severe brain concussion, many broken ribs so that is why you have a hard time breathing and mustn't talk. They crushed your testicles so you'll never be able to father children. That is the only irreparable damage they did. You are bruised over every inch of your body, but we can't find any broken bones. Now just drink this chicken soup and rest."

"Does Ashley know I'm here?," I inquired.

"That boy with the bitter warped nature can only get in here over my dead body. He is guilty of all *seven* deadly sins."

When I heard the word *seven* a chill went over my entire body. I finished two bowls of soup and then asked "How long have I been here?"

"Today will be your third day," she smiled. "Now go to sleep."

My awakening was an entry into a new world. Aunt Mae proved to be my teacher, confidante, healer, advisor and spiritual director. She assured me that my moral values were proper but that I must learn of the spiritual values as an educated Christian. This was all foreign to me but I was captivated by her soft spoken, self assured ways and her resemblance to my own mother whom I hadn't seen since I was ten years old. Aunt Mae was a house slave for a Reverend and Mrs. Bell who had no children. They treated her kindly and taught her to read, write and live according to Christian principles. When they both died, they gave her a tidy sum of money and her freedom. The Jowerses knew of her talents and hired her to be in charge and train the house slaves. She said she was aware of Poku's demise and the details of her "sudden illness."

When I told her of my encounter with the light, Poku and my father, she wept. She said she understood perfectly and interpreted the vision for me. That experience was to be the threshold to my world of Christianity. She also told me to always remember that my people back home were probably better people than many Christians she had met and that I would also encounter. "Just because you see a rat in the potato bin, doesn't make it a potato." I later discovered the significance of that statement.

Between lessons on the alphabet and basic arithmetic, I would tell about my cousins Kweku and Poku. She couldn't understand why I suppressed my love for Poku but I had no answer. Maybe it was because of my primary role as protector that I let it overshadow my emotions. I believe Poku could see deep within me and understood how I truly felt.

My lessons about God, His Son and Spirit and the history of creation fascinated me to the point that I pushed for her to go on even after she grew tired. Everything that I had thought about this earth seemed to fall into place with her teachings. It was a confirmation of my own ideas of this world and its people. I was captivated by her revelation of the body, mind, soul and spirit. To me this life seemed to be more purposeful than just living and dying as my family had thought. If I could just return to them and tell them of this new understanding!

Once I was able to sit up, Aunt Mae brought me a book with children's stories. I was amazed how the letters became words and the words became sentences. Numbers added up the same way to a magical total. I just had to learn more.

My schooling came to an abrupt halt when Master Ashley found that I was able to sit up. He ordered me out to the gin shed where I could sit on a high stool and run the gin. The letters 'York, Penna' now meant something to me for now I could read.

When the superintendent of the mill discovered that I could read and was good with numbers, he gave me the job as weigh master handling the tobacco and cotton crop. This gave me a chance to heal my sore muscles and learn more about processing cotton and tobacco. I practiced my printing every chance I would get, even with a stick in the dirt. The other slaves thought I was a show-off intellectual.

■ ■ ■ ■ ■ ■ ■ ■ ■ ■

As the years went by, season by season, my love and devotion for Aunt Mae grew. I told her of my quest for freedom but she advised me not to make another near fatal mistake but to do it with much more forethought and preparation. She told me of the many factors that went into a successful escape. The route of the underground railway was the way north and to freedom. My naiveté was an honorable trait but could be my downfall on the road in search of freedom. People with no scruples were too eager to earn an extra dollar for turning in a runaway for a paltry reward. "You must be able to read people and look deep into their souls," she would say. "A blind person can detect a scoundrel better than one with all five senses because they listened intently and were not distracted by their appearance," she would counsel me. Be aware but do not be cynical was her adage.

Runaways were a regular event on the plantation due to the cruel treatment and the high number of slaves. There were a little over one hundred on the Jowers plantation. Ashley's domination over me eased up after I survived his beating. When Kweku and I fatally wounded an animal and it continued to charge us, we were more than frightened, therefore Ashley now knows that I am capable of surviving and able to do him harm.

Our evenings were taken up with spiritual and folk songs or else we would listen to Aunt Mae teach us from the Bible. Although we were illiterate, most of us were eager to learn. I learned to read and understand simple words but could only write in block letters with poor spelling, so I just write an 'X' instead of spelling out my name.

Ashley's four lackeys were always present when there was trouble. One night after a drinking bout with hard cider, Race and Snakey got into a knife fight. As the other two looked on and urged them to fight to the end, Snakey finally dropped from the loss of blood. They carried Race to Aunt Mae's cabin and had her patch him up but it was too late for Snakey. Aunt Mae bandaged Race as best she could and then ordered him out of her cabin for she felt a satanic presence. She told me that he was the most evil person she had ever encountered.

The lackeys were free to sleep when they wanted and move about as they wished as long as they were available to Ashley when he needed them. When they were not out chasing runaways, they would rouse a slave out of his sleep and give him a head start across the field and then get the hounds out, just to give them training. When the dogs got to the man first, they would attack him until the searchers would arrive. By then many a man would be badly mauled. This was amusement for the lackeys for they considered their practice a total success.

My life took a turn for the best one night or might I say, an answer to my prayer when a field hand came to my cabin and said there was a slave from the neighboring plantation who was asking for me by the road gate. Being a bit suspicious by this time, I took an old wheel spoke with me in case it was a ruse. When I approached the figure I recognized the silhouette of my cousin Kweku.

"Kweku?," I asked hesitantly.

"Yes, Kinga," he answered. "It is I."

I swung open the gate and embraced him in a near violent manner. It was like meeting someone from the dead.

He explained how he walked off the Mepkin plantation and headed for Charleston. Master Mepkin had himself been a prisoner in England so he treated us in a kindly manner and refused to brand us so I was able to leave quite easily. Master Paisley discovered me in

Charleston and recaptured me. Being an unscrupulous person, he opted to sell me the second time. When I inquired as to your whereabouts, he said he would sell me to the Hay plantation bordering the Jowers place. That way we could see each other.

All the events since our parting poured out like a dam that breached its breast. The murder of Poku, my attempt to flee north and my near fatal beating by Ashley and his sadistic henchmen. I told of my encounter with Poku in another world but he could not understand, just as he had a hard time comprehending my Master Love and my immortal soul.

"Our souls are knotted together," I told him, "and freedom is within our grasp." I went on to explain what Aunt Mae had told me about a successful way of escape by means of the underground railway. He agreed that we should make such plans for the future.

Kweku told of his experiences as a slave in this broad new land. Master Mepkin had treated him kindly and also his new master Ronald Hay. He was very content with his trusting master who treated him as though he were an extended family member. Master Hay's son had just returned from war in Louisiana where he was slightly wounded in the battle of New Orleans. He brought with him a family of slaves who were quadroons, only one-fourth black. This family had the same color and features of our own family in Africa. Kweku felt a special bonding to these people.

We made plans to meet regularly after dark by this same gate that closed off a main artery to the next town. Jowers permitted neighbors to use this shorter route at their discretion provided all trespassers closed the gate behind them. The road went by our shipping shed platform where the scales were set up for the weighing of cotton and tobacco and where I spent much of my time. When any other persons were about we agreed to only speak Swahili, just as though we had our own private code!

I hugged my cousin goodnight and told him how much I had missed his companionship. He offered to kill Ashley for me but I told him he would have to learn to control his anger. Time would be our friend.

"Oh, by the way, cousin. What war are you talking about?"

"They call it the war of 1812. They say the worst of it was fought up north. It was between this land and England."

I walked away more confused than ever about the "war."

CAMBRIA TRIBUNE
Thursday, November 30, 1860
EIGHTH DAY STORY

*A*unt Mae kept after me to study and improve myself
every free hour I had. I asked her, "If Ashley is out to
prove brain can overcome strength and I am smarter and
stronger than he is, why is he still in charge of me?"

"Brain does overcome brawn," Aunt Mae answered.
"Couldn't we capture a powerful lion by digging a pit and
killing him when he fell in?"

"Yes," I answered, "but..."

"There is something that you must learn is more
powerful than brain and brawn and that is money. Ashley
has money to buy and sell people, guns, animals and most
anything. He is more crafty than he is smart. I must warn
you, he keeps a double shot derringer hidden on himself at
all times. So beware!"

I thanked her for telling me and then she turned to
another subject. She wanted to make me a new clean shirt
so I could meet my friend Kweku in dignity. As she was
taking my measurements, she became curious about my
height. Standing on a chair, she made a mark on the wall
level with the top of my head. Then she had me hold her
tape to the mark and she knelt on the floor and shouted,
"My lands! Seven feet, two inches! Boy, when are you
going to stop growing?"

Aunt Mae's gentleness was offset by the gruff and
overbearing task master slave "Robu." He gained favors by

keeping evil alive on the plantation; Aunt Mae said he had sold his soul to the devil.

Robu assigned me to the conjugal cabin for a week. This was my first experience so my cabin mates filled me in with the procedure. The healthiest and strongest slaves were ordered to cohabit with the healthiest women. This would produce good, strong children who would make good workers. If the woman was attractive, the white men would assume she was pregnant so they would cohabit with them for their pleasure.

The conjugal cabin was clean with a large double bed and clean blankets. There were candles on stands on both sides of the bed. Testing the bed, I found it to be of the same soft and comfortable quality as Aunt Mae's bed.

As I sat there in the flickering light, the door flew open and Robu thrust a young black frightened girl into the room. He told us we had one week to get a baby started and then slammed the door shut and left us to ourselves.

I asked the shaking girl what her name was and she answered "Julie" in a quivering childish voice.

"Don't be frightened, child" I assured her as my thoughts turned to Poku. "Nobody is going to hurt you in here."

I told her that I was incapable of producing children but we could take advantage of the nice soft clean bed for a week. She could sleep on one side and I on the other and she would be safe and no one would have to know that we would remain celibate. She laughed and cried at the same time for my height was quite intimidating.

We blew out the candles and I told her of my cousin Poku and she said she had known her and admired her greatly. I asked her how old she was and she figured about fifteen years. That made me angry for we did not even breed our animals back home until they were fully matured. Sleep did not come easily.

When I told Aunt Mae of my new cabin she gave me some advice. "That girl is going to be in trouble if they find out after a week with you she is still a virgin. I will have to visit her and artificially deprive her of her maiden head." She then explained to me what she was referring to and then I understood perfectly. Any way we could foil the Jowerses' sinister plans gave me great satisfaction. Aunt Mae had a good hearty laugh at the ruse we would carry on for a week.

Kweku and I missed very few evening meetings at the gate. He shared his experiences at the Hay plantation and I shared my new venture into education. On one visit he showed up with a large pair of boots that were too large for anyone on their plantation. They came with a large order of boots of various sizes. Those boots were the first real footwear I had ever worn. They seemed so heavy at the time.

Hay was shipping a wagon load of pine to the next town and Kweku said he got the job of delivering the lumber and to be on the lookout for him. It was only the older trusted slaves who ever got such a responsible position but Kweku was chosen for he stood out so obviously above all others.

It was a little after noon that I heard the gate swing open with its usual creaking and scraping and there sat Kweku high and mighty on top of a load of rough lumber pulled by a team of black mules. The young girl in the wide brimmed hat attending the gate was of greater attraction. She had long black glistening hair over her shoulders and a slim trim figure. When she caught me staring she smiled and waved to me. Kweku had told her about me. When she closed the gate behind the wagon, she climbed up on the front wheel and then up on top of the load beside Kweku. He held his head high and waved in a flaunting manner just as though he owned the whole rig.

Curiosity was getting the better of me and I could hardly wait to meet at the gate that evening. As he approached he held his hand high and said "I know just what you're going to ask." Then he proceeded to explain that his helper was one of the slaves brought up from Louisiana, a quadroon named Jenny. He was inquisitive as to why I was interested in a farm hand from his plantation. Of course he was saying that with tongue in cheek. I told him that I was moved and impressed by her smile, beauty and stature. Kweku said he would pass the compliment on.

Aunt Mae was a driving force on the plantation. She was a living symbol of freedom but instead of resting and relaxing, she was a bundle of energy trying to improve the life of the captive workers. In her assertive and positive way, she was able to get all the slaves who were to be baptized free from work one Sunday morning.

An itinerant preacher up from Monck's Corner was there at the swimming hole that morning. There were about thirty of us from the Jowers and nearby plantations to receive the sacrament of baptism. Kweku, Jenny and two other field hands showed up to watch the ceremony.

The preacher started off by giving us a teaching on our entry into the Christian world. He said we would be transformed from children of slave masters to children of God. There I stood, seven feet two, two hundred and eighty pounds, and I'm called a child, twenty-five years old. I had mixed feelings about being the largest man there and yet in a childish setting. Aunt Mae came over to me and put her arms around my waist, telling me how proud she was of me and called me her "iron butterfly." She said

I looked much better than when she rescued me with her broom stick. We had a mutual admiration.

After our immersion in the water, the preacher asked any of the onlookers if any of them would choose to leave the heathen world and be born again. He encouraged them by explaining the new life with Jesus as our brother and master. Many were moved by the short sermon and at least eight more men stepped forward, including Kweku and Jenny, too. Aunt Mae announced that all were welcome to our evening singing and bible studies and that drew a hardy applause.

Now that we were baptized we were warned to leave the old behind and put on the new person so that at no time would we be an embarrassment to our fellow Christians or a disappointment to our Lord God.

I eventually discovered that this new found religion was not solely a white man's theology but it was meant for the entire world, respecting all peoples. My daily drudgery was now a consecration to God and a task of glory. I felt an inner strength that I never knew possible and Kweku said I was a different person than the one he had previously known. I gave credit to Aunt Mae for saving my body and my soul and putting this new fire into my life.

Plans for my new bid for freedom began to take shape. Kweku said I should go alone for two reasons. One person had a better chance to slip by without detection and he was enjoying his new life with the Hays. He did promise to join me later on so that we could spend our last years together. Aunt Mae suggested that I wait until the following summer and travel during the *seventh* month. Like a good Mother, she asked to be the one who would do the planning and the packing of the necessary gear. I knew of no other who was so knowledgeable of the underground route. She also had me repeat the word "abolitionist" over and over again so that I would know what it meant when I heard it.

Since no more slaves arrived in the south after 1808, we were becoming more valuable each day. As the old field hands and house servants died off, the plantations became shorthanded. Horses, mules and machinery did the bulk of the work. Harvesting the crops could only be done by hand so it started to cost more and profits went down. The exploitation of human beings was a black mark on the civilized society and there were movements in the north to prohibit it completely. Aunt Mae had me memorize the word "Quaker" for that meant help.

The one night that is branded in my mind is the night Kweku showed up at the gate with another person. When he said he had a surprise for me, I had a faint idea what he meant. Then he said, "Cousin, this is Jenny, my helper." Even by the faint light of the quarter moon, I could see her handsome features. My God, she was beautiful.

The nights that Kweku said he would not be able to meet me I asked if he could send Jenny instead. He gave a hearty laugh and slapped me on my back. "Yes, yes, of course, cousin."

Jenny and I had a lot in common. We talked incessantly of our past and especially of our future. I asked her if she cared to come to our singing and prayer meetings and she said she would like it very much since she knew me and she was quite shy. As time went on, we developed a bonding in body and soul. Because she was so shy but wanted to be a good Christian, Aunt Mae suggested that I quote Romans 16:16 from the bible to her and then practice what it says. When I asked, Aunt Mae quoted, "Greet one another with a holy hug or kiss." I used the bible faithfully thereafter.

With my new found religion and my love for Jenny growing, I found it much easier to get up at daybreak and go to work. Life now gave me a definite goal and my imagination was overworked with ideas for the future. If I could get to the north by August, find work and build a cabin, then Jenny and I could marry. When I confided in her that I was unable to produce a child, she responded in a happy voice, "Then we'll raise someone else's." Aunt Mae's saying "Man can endure anything as long as he has hope" took on a whole new meaning.

CAMBRIA TRIBUNE
Saturday, December 1, 1860
NINTH DAY STORY

M y days were boring in so far as my work was concerned. My immediate supervisor was pleased with my work but Ashley always found fault with my weights or my figures. Just from his own observations he would accuse me of underweighing the bales and when I tried to defend my accuracy he would order me to shut up. He could ruin everyone's day by his self-righteousness.

The brightest point of my day would occur when I could look out and see Kweku and Jenny pass by on their freight wagon. Kweku sat high on the seat looking like a king driving his golden chariot with beautiful Jenny sitting by his side. He would shout to me, "Tutaonana usiku huu!" (See you tonight) and I would answer "Ndio" (Yes). Jenny would take off her wide brim hat and wave to me but it was her enchanting smile that made me proud. I sensed that she loved me as much as I loved her but she hadn't spoken openly about it.

Down deep inside I was fighting a battle. One night after a bible study on forgiveness, I called Aunt Mae aside and confided that I had hatred in my heart. She asked me to explain, so I told her that I could not forgive Ashley for killing Poku when she fought off his advances and I could not forgive him for having his henchmen nearly beat me to death. Here I took time to thank Aunt Mae for intervening. I held no grudge against the four attackers for they were savages who had no common sense and were merely Ashley's puppets.

Clasping my face between her two hands she looked directly into my eyes, for I was sitting on a low box, and said, "My little boy, I can understand your anger. Ashley not only robbed you of your beloved but he tortured her and killed her. Retribution will be forthcoming by our Lord and we can have no part in it. As for his attack on you, that was for more than just running away. Your size is intimidating to his puny body. And besides, his father is also to share the blame for he goads his son into mistreating those who are bigger to prove that his brain is more powerful and can subdue your strength. He is wrong on all counts. You are a prudent person endowed with good old fashioned common sense and combined with your size and strength you overwhelm the boy. He is both envious and jealous so he is obsessed with hurting you. Of course it is difficult for you to placate your anger and find forgiveness in your heart, but you must strive to survive. Acid does more harm to the container than anything on the outside and this hatred is like an acid within you. Pray for him and you will be heaping hot coals upon his head. I know this because that is what the Good Book says, Romans 12:20."

"Son, you know by now that life is not easy and is not going to ever be a bed of roses but if you run a good race you will be rewarded with a huge manor house in heaven. Now, let's you and me ask God for forgiveness."

That was my Aunt Mae, a woman sent by God to bring glad tidings to the lowly, to heal the broken hearted, to proclaim freedom to the captives and release to the slaves. I firmly believe that Poku was within that woman, maybe Poku was her spirit. I do not know. How I survived can only be attributed to my Master Love and it was that faith that made it possible for me to tell you this story of my life. I hope in telling my story to you that someone reading it might be lifted out of darkness and into the light as I was.

Kweku enjoyed his life with the Hay family so he was not as impressed with his new life as a Christian as I was. He was always a good living man but I wanted him and also Jenny to experience the euphoric sensation of basking in the glory of God. Ever since I was kidnapped at the age of ten, I knew nothing but sadness and heartache, and now I was born again into a new Kingdom. This did not give me mere hope; it gave me assurance that I was going to survive and come into a whole new world of peace and love. Jenny was there and I was to carry her as a bride over the threshold into a new life.

In the Spring of 1816, I started to make serious plans for my final break for freedom. Aunt Mae stood at the heart of the situation. She was a member of the underground serving on the southern end. It was a clandestine organization. They had their own esoteric vocabulary and signs, not only to protect the runaways, but also to protect themselves from very hostile neighbors. A slave from the first day he is able to work to the last of his working days is worth his weight in gold.

Aunt Mae wrote letters to accomplices in North Carolina, Virginia, West Virginia and Pennsylvania gathering all the information she could glean for a safe route and safe havens for layovers and provisions. There were many fanatical abolitionists who would risk their lives and property to set the black people free. By the month of June, she spoke to me late in the evening out in the open field. She was aware of those of our own race who would trade any information for whatever favors they could get. She warned me not to do a thing out of my normal routine so as to arouse suspicion. She had my rucksack all packed except for the food which she would fill in at the last moment. The almanac gave the month of July as the best time for the full moon between the longest stations. I was to tell no one but Kweku and Jenny. I hugged Aunt Mae goodnight with mixed feelings. July was the *seventh* month!

Two nights later, I met Kweku and Jenny at the gate. As we lay low in the grass, I told them of the plans Aunt Mae and I had laid out. Jenny squeezed my hand and began to cry. I told her to be patient for nothing in the world could separate us for we were already as one. Kweku said he would do his part in delivering her to me as soon as I got settled in the north. Jenny drew her strength from the two of us and her new found Savior. It was agreed that I was to leave the first of July.

The following day as Kweku drove by he shouted in Swahili, "I have a thought to share with you tonight." Those on the weighing platform asked me what he said.

"He said, 'Those are good looking friends you have there.'" They were very pleased with the translation.

That night after the singing and the prayer meeting, Kweku, Jenny and I went out by the gate and laid in the grass. Kweku said that the mill had a shipment of clear pine of molding stock, to go to the molding mill at Lumberton leaving June 30th. He had the idea of loading the light dry lumber with a cavity in the center where I would hide. The bed of the freight wagon is just a framework so I would have ingress and egress above the reach pole. I would be safe, have food and drink and with Kweku driving he would give me a chance to climb out when the horses watered. The load would be covered by a canvas tarpaulin for molding stock could not get wet. This would also keep me dry.

I thanked my cousin for the good planning and told Aunt Mae of the new scheme. She said a day earlier would not make that much difference, in fact it would help Mrs. Borda in Lumberton prepare me for my next station in Southern Pines, another lumber village. Jenny asked if she could go along as a helper, but Kweku said it would be up to Master Ronald to make that decision.

The next few weeks moved as slow as months and I took care not to whistle or sing more than I ordinarily do. I did get to meet Jeff, a quadroon who accompanied Jenny and Master Mays up from Louisiana. He was a happy soul who could play the mouth harp and sing all the Cajun songs. The one song I'll never forget till the day I die, for I sing it each day.

> *"Oh, my pretty quadroon,*
> *My flower that faded too soon.*
> *My heart's like the strings on my banjo,*
> *All broke for my pretty quadroon."*

I'll be forever grateful to the person who wrote that song for it kept my Jenny alive in my mind all the way north on that long dark trail.

June 29, 1816 is a date burned into my brain. Aunt Mae canceled Bible study for she said she wasn't feeling well. I went to her cabin and she pulled me inside after she turned down her lamp. I entered the dark room and after closing the door she then turned the lamps up. The shades were drawn so it was an eerie setting in this nicely furnished cabin. From under her bed she drew out a double rucksack much like leather saddle bags except this fit over my head and hung in front and back. In it was a compass, an Army waterproof poncho that she got from Master Hay, a thick cotton blanket, four pairs of knit stockings to be worn with my boots and food for three days travel. She had a special unbreakable flask that held a gallon of water except she had it filled with soup. As I sat at her little table, she pulled out of the drawer a beautiful black leather bound bible. There were markers placed throughout the bible except these markers were coded to a map telling me of the underground railroad stations along the way. The scriptures were signed by authors who were actually the owners of the stations. By lifting the facing page, she pulled out a map from South Carolina to Johnstown, Pennsylvania. The first station was Lumberton marked '#1.' On the '#1' book marker was a scripture by Mrs. Borda; the next station was Southern Pines marked '#2' and on that book marker was the name Forristal with a quote from Psalm 119.

The route was marked so clearly that I thought it impossible for me to get lost. I didn't count on rascals turning signs around to confuse runaways; my naiveté was almost my downfall.

Aunt Mae thrust her greatest earthly possession into my hand and said, "Be this bible as a lamp unto thy feet. Neither your body or your soul can go astray if you read this Bible," referring to the map and book markers within.

"I'll probably never see you again in this world, my love. But we will meet again in the next. May God be with you," and with that I bent down and kissed my Godmother good-bye.

"You saved my body and soul from death, Aunt Mae. My gratitude cannot be put into words." Then I went out into the darkness with the rucksack and bible.

Kweku and Jenny were waiting for me. They took me to the other side of the gate where the loaded wagon stood. Crawling on our hands and knees, Kweku showed me where to stow my gear in the cavity he built for me.

Climbing upon the reach pole I slid inside the little hollow. It was perfect. Leaving my gear, I made arrangements to meet them before day break and hide away before they hitched up the team. Jenny was to go along and help Kweku with the transaction at the Lumberton molding mill. I bid them goodnight and slipped back to my cabin.

A nightingale awakened me, so I thought it must be time to be leaving for the birds usually start their singing right before the day breaks. I took my clothes and kente cloth and headed for the gate, the plantation still fast asleep.

Crawling on my stomach under the fence, I found the wagon, mounted the reach pole and snuggled up into my crawl hole. In the quiet of darkness, I drank some of Aunt Mae's soup to the rhythm of the chirping crickets. They were like little guards since at the slightest noise they would stop chirping so their song told me all was well.

As the day broke, I could look down and see the ground taking color. Shortly I could hear the harnessed horses approaching and then Jenny appeared under the wagon and looking up she said, "Here are some warm corn cakes wrapped in molasses, love. You'll need them to start your long journey to our new home." That was the first time I had ever heard her use the word love. It was the right way to start the long trek.

After Kweku had the traces hooked up to the double tree, he crawled under the load as if to check the reach pole. I assured him that all was well and then I heard Jenny open the gate. As we moved through, I thought that it would be about another hour or two that they discover me missing. When I heard the gate close and Jenny climb up on the seat, then I realized that a lifelong dream was about to come true.

Kweku broke the horses into a nice steady trot for the dry white pine was no heavier than the empty wagon. The team would put a good distance between me and the Jowers place in two hours on this level road. The wheels seemed to say, "On your way, on your way" as the iron rims dug into the soft dirt road. Above the sound of the grinding wheels and the trotting horses I could hear Jenny sing a song about Shenandoah. It was music to my ears for she had a beautiful voice with a Cajun accent.

When the wheels stopped, I knew we were at the north gate about to leave the Jowers property. As Jenny dismounted, she asked as if speaking to the ground, "Are you comfortable in there?" I answered that my ride to freedom could not be any nicer.

After we passed through the gate, the thought struck me that Kweku and Jenny could drive all over the country and be trusted just because of good-living owners. If Jowers could just understand that decency pays off, they would not have so much trouble with their servants. The bible is very explicit about how slaves should serve their masters and how masters should treat their slaves. Slavery was not condemned by God; that is a mystery to me.

We were not more than a half hour out of the north gate when I heard fast galloping horses overtaking us. I could only hear so much from my hiding place so Jenny filled me in as to what took place.

Two blacks came riding alongside our team with long whips coiled around their McClelland saddles. One man reached over and grabbed our horse by the bit and pulled him to a stop.

"We're looking for a runaway and he's just about your size."

"Well I'm not your runaway," snaps Kweku. "So get your hand off that bridle right now."

With that the other man was riding to the back of our wagon tapping the tarp with the metal handle of his whip. The mean-faced black let go of the bridle and turned to face them. He uncoiled his whip and slashed it around Kweku's neck, knocking off Jenny's hat in the process. Like a flash of lightening, Kweku grabbed the whip as Jenny grabbed the reins and Kweku gave a hard pull yanking the rider out of the saddle. He fell to the ground with his right foot caught in the stirrup. Kweku pulled in the whip handle and then unwound it from around his neck. He stood up and with the whip raised in the air, he brought it down across the horse's back. The horse shot across the road, over the ditch and through a stand of pines with the screaming fool dragging alongside. The other rider came from behind the wagon and took off through the woods in pursuit of the runaway horse. Coiling up the whip, Kweku handed it to Jenny and taking the reins, said "This is a gift for our passenger."

I debated whether to come out of my hiding place and give Kweku assistance or play it safe and let my cousin vent his anger. Those two lackeys of Ashley's were no match for Kweku for he had no fear of whips. The man was in a safer position with his foot caught in the stirrup of a runaway horse than coming in contact with an angry Kweku. When we pulled off the road at noon to rest and eat, Kweku presented me with his latest trophy, the whip. We sat under the wagon and ate our lunch so I would be able to scramble into my hollow in case somebody came by.

That night we camped by a stream on the outskirts of a village called Dillon. After dark we were able to refresh ourselves in the stream before laying down for a good sleep on the warm June night. Jenny said that this would be the last night we would have together so she cuddled close and laid her head on my shoulder. She feared that she might never see me again once we parted in Lumberton, but I promised her that I would get through and Kweku would bring her to me in the North. She asked if I would take a vow of betrothal and I said nothing would please me more and also would give me strength and a reason to succeed in my quest for a new home of our own across the Mason-Dixon line. With my arm around her, and my hand in hers, I vowed before God and Kweku that I would be wed to her as soon as I could provide a home and care for her. She pledged her life to me saying she would be my mate until death. Kweku clapped his hands softly in agreement and then we decided to go to sleep at the close of that special private ceremony.

I was awakened by the smell of smoke from a blazing campfire. Jenny had a pot of water boiling for some hot tea and she warmed corn bread on a tray resting upon the iron pot. She was so clean and tidy about herself and everything that she did that I knew I would enjoy her Cajun cooking.

We were on our way before the sun peeked over the horizon and the horses were feeling frisky. Kweku gave them their head so I watched as the ground flew by at an exhilarating speed. Then I rolled on my back and looked at the white pine overhead. It looked so pure, flawless and perfect that I thought of what God has created. Then I thought that His greatest creation was Jenny for she was a paragon like Poku. Did God send Jenny to fill the void in my life left by the demise of Poku? Maybe this was one of the ways that Poku had of taking care of me, sending me a helpmate like Jenny.

The sun was setting and the horses were tiring when we met a man going in the opposite direction. I could hear

Kweku ask him how much further to Lumberton. "*Seven more miles*," he answered. I said, "Thank you, Poku."

We pulled into the molding mill yard at dusk. Jenny and Kweku took the directions with them to locate my first station, the home of Mrs. Borda, while I stayed hidden in the lumber. The streets were empty as everybody was in their homes by that hour.

My collaborators returned shortly and showed me that by following the alley from the lumber mill I would come to the Borda house through the back yard. There was a potting shed behind the house and it was there I was to meet my rescuer. I hugged Kweku and then embraced Jenny much more tenderly and vowed that we would be together again. We kissed softly, then I said, "Tutaonana baadaye."

CAMBRIA TRIBUNE
Wednesday, December 6, 1860
TENTH DAY STORY

With my rucksack hanging around my neck, I carefully made my way up the alley till I came to a figure by a wooden gate. "Ben?," she inquired. "Yes," I answered.

Silently, she opened the gate and I followed her to the shed in the backyard. It appeared dark but when she opened the door, I was struck by the light from lamps setting on each side of the room. The room had shelves of pottery of every shape and design and of various colors. They all glistened in the light for they were highly glazed.

Mrs. Borda was a tall, dark-haired woman. She had eyes that sparkled with the joy of being able to save a slave from a life of misery and unending drudgery. She moved about quickly for time was of essence and she seemed a well-organized person.

She took my measurements, she explained that she would sew an outfit for me to wear as Uncle Sam at the Fourth of July celebration. Since the next day was July 2nd, she just had two days to assemble trousers, coat and hat. I was to rest up for the long trip to Southern Pines and let them know what I needed for the trip.

Mr. Borda, Charles she called him, was to drive me in their open business buggy in open daylight, as though we were on our way to a parade or celebration for Independence Day. This, she explained, would probably be the best day of my journey north, riding in comfort at full speed.

Charles came in with a warm pail of vegetable soup with some bread and fruit. He was a short stocky man with short-cropped hair and a warm friendly smile. When he shook my hand, he looked up and said, "How's the weather up there?" For a moment I did not grasp the meaning of his question and then I realized that he was referring to my height. Since my head was just a few inches from the ceiling, it was warmer on my face than what he felt. I thanked him and Mrs. Borda for all the inconvenience I was causing them but they said it was their ministry.

I slept in the pottery shed that night on a cot provided for the likes of me. It was to be just one of the many unique places that I would be using as a sleeping place on my trip north.

The following day I spent with Charles going over my route through the northern states. He was also a very systematic person for he had distance calculated and the approximate time it would take between stations. He already had made up a calendar for me to carry and mark off each day as I progressed. Mrs. Borda had me try on the clothes as she pieced them together.

On the morning of the Fourth, we arose very early and had a good meal. I was then dressed in trousers with white and red stripes going from my waist to my feet. The jacket was made from flags using only the white stars on a blue background. The hat was a scull cap of red, white and blue. Then they covered all of my dark skin with a white grease paint. Loose fitting white gloves covered my hands. Mrs. Borda was overjoyed with the finished product for it made me appear even taller than I actually was.

Charles put my rucksack in the back of a buggy that he had decorated with flags flying from all four corners of the canopy. Mrs. Borda told me of the food she had put in my rucksack and then gave me her blessing. As we drove down the street, I saw her waving until we were out of sight. It was a colorful sight for anyone to behold.

The team was a pair of matched sorrel Morgan mares with much stamina and grace. We flew out into the open country and would be well on our way by the time the sun would come up. Charles offered me a drink of brandy from his flask but I declined for I knew the evils from overindulgence.

There were farms scattered throughout the countryside and I had my first experience of what it is like to be traveling in the open in full daylight as a free person. I also realized that even in Pennsylvania I would be continually looking over my shoulder for bounty hunters.

People along the way assumed that we were on our way to a parade. As we went full speed down the road, Charles recognized the Lumberton stage approaching. It was a four seated open hackney full of Fourth of July celebrators. When they caught sight of our buggy, they stopped along the road and waited for us. Charles asked me to release the wing nut on the canopy and as he released his side, the top lowered. He reigned our team to slow trot and had me stand up supporting myself with one hand on the lower top and the other on the buggy whip upright in its receptacle.

The passengers stood alongside the road waving their flags as I stood upright as a statue. My colorful striped costume with my long swallow tailed coat reaching to the back of my knees made me appear much taller than I was. They cheered in a very festive mood which was obviously bolstered with a bit of alcoholic beverage. I bowed to them and waved them good-bye.

We were both pleased, first by the wonderful job done by Mrs. Borda on my costume and the fact that a runaway could pass scrutiny in such a deceptive manner. We raised the canopy and proceeded at our fast pace.

I reverted to a pensive mood, remembering my conversation with Mrs. Borda. When I spoke in a pessimistic mood of the long hard trip I had ahead, she reprimanded me with the challenge that freedom does not come without a price.

"Forty years ago many men gave up their lives and others lost their families and fortunes to attain the freedom that you now seek. Your trip of a few hundred miles is no comparison to what others have suffered. You should ask forgiveness of God and the souls of the dead patriots whom you have just slighted." Mrs. Borda was a very religious and dedicated woman who put her beliefs into action by sacrificing all earthly possessions and even imprisonment to help us less fortunate human beings. I took time to myself to ask forgiveness and then turn to Charles and say thank you. He said, "For what?"

I answered, "For more than I can say on our short trip this day."

At noon our horses were covered with lather so it was at this time that Charles pulled into a farmyard owned by a friend he just called 'Dave.' He asked me to stay in the buggy while he made a deal with his friend who might not feel too kindly about abetting an escape plan.

While I ate my lunch, Charles went to the house to see his friend. He returned with the news that Dave had influenza but he would loan me his team for our trip into Southern Pines. He unhitched our team and took them to the barn and then brought out a pair of small jacks that looked mighty frisky and hadn't been out of the barn for a spell. As he hitched the jacks to the double tree, I asked what was the significance of the costume.

"Well, during this last war with England, a meat inspector by the name of Sam Wilson put his initials on all the meat. Some people up north who opposed the war started the nickname 'Uncle Sam.' Now people are giving their impressions of how this fictitious character should look and my wife suggested using the material from some flags. It seems appropriate and acceptable. Do you understand what I'm saying?"

I understood perfectly and it all made sense for I had heard the term 'John Bull' used to denote the English.

The jacks were so lively that I thanked God that they agreed to go in the same direction. They took the bit in their teeth and Charles gave them their head. We had a wild ride into Southern Pines. People all thought we were coming from a parade but they still had enough enthusiasm to give us a big flag waving ovation.

Charles walked the jacks to the other edge of town and then pulled into a residential yard where the sign 'Tile' was displayed.

A black curly haired man came out to greet us in a sailor uniform. He was of trim figure so he stood proudly in his nautical outfit bedecked with ribbons. Before speaking a word, he took the bridle of one jack and led the rig in behind his shop, well out of public view.

Although it was getting quite dark, he was very cautious.

"Lawrence, I want you to meet the new Ben David. Although he is a very smart man, he still doesn't have enough sense to know when to stop growing and now everybody is afraid to tell him."

We all had a good laugh for despite my size, I never meant to ever intimidate anybody. We all pitched in to unharness the horses and lead them to Mr. Forristal's barn.

After watering and feeding the subdued Jacks, we went to the house to meet Mrs. Forristal.

Those people all seemed to be of one peerage, all good living, down to earth people. Aunt Mae, the Bordas and now the Forristals all seemed to be of one mold; they were all good living Christians.

Helen Forristal proceeded to strip me to the waist and remove all the white grease paint and then had me change into my regular clothes. She said she would keep the Uncle Sam outfit for posterity so they would have something to show their grandchildren how slavery was defeated. They were all so dedicated and committed that they knew that in time it would be abolished for it had already happened in England.

Lawrence was a tile man who sold and set tile for a living so he had a shop not unlike Mrs. Borda's. There was a cot set up for me there so no visitors to the house might catch me there. The cot was too short so I made a bed on the wooden floor with the blankets I had there. The pillow was of duck down and the softest I had ever used. The day ended on a serene note for Mrs. Forristal was a wonderful cook and made sure no one left the table still wanting.

I bid Charles farewell in the morning for he had the long trip back to Lumberton alone. He gave me the four flags from his buggy to remember him by and to fly them every fourth of July thereafter. I thanked him from the bottom of my heart for that was the only truly comfortable trip I would have on my trek north.

Lawrence and Helen Forristal had me rest up all day for I was to leave at dusk for a night trip on my way to Sanford. I rested by sitting in the tile shop answering questions from the Forristals while she sewed me a new shirt with long sleeves for my fall arrival in Pennsylvania.

They were very curious about my childhood, my trip to the Gold Coast and then my voyage to South Carolina.

I could not help notice their interest in my story concerning Poku speaking to me from the grave. Their concern heightened when I mentioned the word *'seba'* as a sign of her presence, for they had planned to change my route formally designated to county road *seven*. It was a road less traveled with only one town between Southern Pines and Sanford, that consisted of a store and post office known as Pumptown because of a handpump and watering trough.

The reason for the route change was revealed when Lawrence produced a wanted poster of me with a true likeness drawn of me and the name 'Dolt Jowers, $ 1 000 reward.' They said the highest reward they had ever seen was five hundred dollars, so the area would have many bounty hunters and to trust no one, especially of my own color. Many slaves were promoted to plush jobs such as coachman, footman or house servants for turning in a runaway. I was more angered at the name, for Dolt stood for stupid and Jowers reeked of evil. Ben David was my name and I would answer to no other.

They warned me that the rest of my trip through Carolina would probably be my most dangerous, for it would be mostly night travel and few underground stations. I was considered double jeopardy for my color distinguished me but my height was most conspicuous.

For supper we had a feast of hickory smoked ham and freshly made egg noodle soup and rye bread. What king could sit at a better table. Mrs. Forristal was an outstanding cook. After feasting, she packed me a bundle of sandwiches and put hot soup in my bottle.

When the sun finally went down they both stood above me on the stoop as I stood with my rucksack hanging over my chest and back. Mrs. Forristal placed her hands on my head and Lawrence put his hands on my shoulders as they gave me their blessing and asked God to deliver me safely from all harm and that I could eventually live in freedom and give God glory for my deliverance.

Lawrence went outside to see that all was clear and then he led me out and accompanied me to the county road to Sanford which was approximately 25 to 30 miles away. He gave me a parting hug and said "May God be with you."

I walked in silence in step with some tree frogs chirping their love calls and very deep in thought. What was my Jenny doing at this time and was Kweku taking good care of her? Then I began to plan the little home I would build. It had to be of adobe brick like the one Chief Asmak had. Ah, I thought, where is that sadistic chief now? How does he like his new role as a common slave like the rest of us? He was truly a coward beneath all that regal facade but fate has a way of coming full circle and enveloping you in the end. Evil begets evil, I said to myself.

Just as I was rounding a bend in the road, I heard galloping horses and wagon wheels approaching behind me. I dived behind a huge oak tree and saw an express wagon drawing near with two lanterns hanging from the two top corners. It was the mail wagon going to Sanford. When it barely got past me, I darted at full speed and grabbed the lowered endgate. With an extra effort, I swung myself up on the seat and settled down for a nice ride in the dark. I could hear the driver when he sang at times and then when he cursed his horses for not keeping their single trees even, causing one horse to carry most of the load. It seemed he had a horse that lagged a bit for he was constantly urging it to step up.

After a few hours, the rig slowed to a walk and we stopped at the post office. I waited until he went in to unlock the door and I slipped across the road and laid in the ditch. While he unloaded his mail, I ate my sandwich and had some soup. The driver also took his break for he was a while coming out.

As he pulled out of Pumptown, I ran behind and took up my position as rear guard. This wagon was a bonus and then again wasn't this county road?

When I saw that day was beginning to break, I jumped off the mail wagon and hit the ditch, in case the driver was looking back. When he was out of sight, I began to look for a place to lay low for the day. I was just on the outskirts of Sanford. The safest place was to go deep in the woods and find a place where I could conceal myself beneath some brush. The weather looked threatening so I took out my poncho and covered myself in case it rained while I slept.

CAMBRIA TRIBUNE
Thursday, December 14, 1860
ELEVENTH DAY STORY

Resting securely under some branches and elder bushes, I crawled beneath my poncho and laid my head on my rucksack. First a few streaks of lightening crossed the dawn sky followed by some far off thunder rumblings. Then one by one I could hear drops of rain fall on the leaves outside my hideaway. It was a soothing natural sound to me that lulled me into a deep sleep, for I was one day closer to freedom than the day before.

In my sleep, I dreamed that a sharp branch was jabbing me in the leg, so I rolled away, but the jabbing continued. I opened my eyes and looked out to see a pair of pant legs only two feet away. Peering out from under my shelter, I saw a muscular man with long, black hair, bare to the waist and of a complexion closely resembling my color. He warned me to stay down while he could question me as he held the upper hand. He asked directly if I were wanted and I said yes, but not wanted as badly as I wanted to get north to freedom. I assured him that I was a peaceful man and had never harmed anyone. With that he asked me to get up to see if I had a weapon. I had none, but he had a long painted knife in his belt and a cross bow in his hand. Then he said, "My name is Jeb and I am also considered sub-human. My mother is of the Catawba Indian tribe and my father who I never knew was white, so I am what you call a half-breed, totally unaccepted by the people here in Sanford."

As we shook hands, he remarked that I was the biggest man he had ever met and asked my age.

"This year I should be twenty-six, or near to it, but when I cross the Mason-Dixon line then I'll start my age from there."

He understood me to be sincere and asked me to go back deeper into the woods to his home. It was made of slash from a mill, that is the first slabs of wood cut from a log. They are covered on one side with bark so are of little value. He showed me how he made two walls of slash nearly a foot apart and then filled the space in between with sawdust. "It's cool in the summer and warm in the winter but isn't too much to look at," he commented.

As we stomped our muddy feet off on the grass outside, a young black girl came to the door.

"Liz, look what I found instead of a wild turkey. What are we going to do with him?," she laughed.

"Let's start by feeding him a good catfish dinner," she answered.

They told me their life story, but the saddest part was Liz's story. When she ran away, no one ever seemed to search for her, so she felt disappointed that no one considered her of any value. Then the life in an isolated cabin in the woods, with Jeb as the only human she ever saw, was not much of an improvement over her life as a slave in the cotton field. She was a very angry person and I could understand, but Jeb was of a different temperament; he simply ignored her needs for he was a provider and he accepted her as a wife.

The crossbow was the work of the cabinet maker and blacksmith combined. They gave Jeb the weapon for they wanted to make one more powerful. Jeb said he could almost put an arrow completely through a deer at close range. In the winter, he survived by running trap lines, then selling the skins and eating the meat. He was very happy living by his wits and what nature provided.

After a good hearty meal of cornpone and catfish, Jeb suggested that he lead me off in the direction of Siler City. I was too much for Liz's two year old mare, so he said I could take his mule and he would ride the pony.

On my journey north, I encountered people of all walks of life but this was a unique couple. They showed me that we need more than just each other, we need friends and community in order to live a full life and learn how to relate.

Liz fixed me a large bag of jerky to chew on as we rode north and gave Jeb a bottle of his favorite apple wine. He said he preferred riding on an empty stomach. We were able to leave before darkness set in, for we were well off any popular route. The leaves still dripped water on my poncho, but Jeb rode bare chested with his long black hair flying in the wind. My mule named 'Maude' could not keep up with the pony, so Jeb more or less intentionally rode ahead so as to clear the trail for me. He said bounty hunters did not like to be this far off the usual route of runaways.

We only stopped once during the night to rest the animals and let them drink and graze a bit. He told me that the story of the Catawba people did not differ too much in hardship from my own life. They had not been brought in by ship, but they were looked upon as lower life and that hurt him badly. He felt as though the invaders had stolen their homes and then turned them out of their lives. I gave him my opinion that the earth had enough for all of us, but greed seemed to always enter the situation.

That good man rode with me all night through woods and fields, skirting the farms and roads to get me to a safe place for the day. We covered thirty miles or more when I stopped at a pile of fence rails as it broke daylight. He helped me build a shelter of the old posts that had been there for years, but had been abandoned for one reason or another.

He ate one of my smoked ham sandwiches with me and washed it down with his apple wine. He then mounted the mule and rode off leading the pony. I expected a good-bye, handshake or a wave, but in his very stoic manner, without letting me thank him, he took off for his full day ride home.

As I settled into my hiding place, I pondered people like Jeb and Liz. They had nothing but two animals and some food they gleaned from nature and yet they shared it all just to help me get north. If only the Jowerses had a fraction of their goodness, it would be a better world.

I woke with an appetite and to the sound of a barking dog in a distant field. The sound was so far off I was not concerned. After satisfying my hunger, I decided to use the low hanging fog as a cover to make a few extra miles before darkness. It looked as though I would be in for a rainy trip on that leg of my journey.

My compass showed due North with Siler City off to my right, so I took advantage of a freshly harvested field of hay as an easy route. Suddenly ahead of me a man on horseback appeared coming up over a rise. Dropping prostrate on the ground, I took the chance of him going off in a different direction for the new cut field provided no protection whatsoever. With my face buried in the wet grass, I held my breath but I could hear the horse's hoofs thumping the earth, reverberating in my body. The horse stopped beside me and a voice said, "Are you sick or are you dead?"

I'm just on my way north and I thought you might be the law."

"No, I'm out looking for my black and white Jersey cow. Did you happen to see it?"

I told him I saw no cow and would it be alright to cut through his field. He then introduced himself as Franck Shuman and told me that with a storm moving in, it would be best that I spend the night in his barn in safety, away from the law. I studied his small dark face for some assurance of truth and honesty, but all I could see was a faint smile. Standing almost against his horse, I was eye level with his upper arm deciding what I should do next, for my bid for freedom depended on my next move.

As he held the reins in his left hand, I spotted a silver bracelet on his left wrist and on the plate was engraved the Star of David. Having studied the Old Testament with Aunt Mae, I knew that the Jews were God's chosen people and my favorite prophets were Isaiah, Jeremiah and Ezekiel, all good Jews. Besides, Aunt Mae said that to be a good Christian, one had to first be a good Jew.

"My name is Ben David," I said. "I'll graciously accept your offer."

He directed me to his barn while he made a further search for his cow. We both arrived at the barn at nearly the same time, but I could see by the steam coming from his horse that he had ridden hard. He took me into his barn and placing a long wooden ladder against the loft, he led me up into his hay mow. Showing me a good bedding spot on the side adjacent to his house, he offered me a horse blanket to cover the straw and make a more comfortable bed. He offered me no food, just descended the ladder and departed.

The rain was coming down heavier as it got darker and I could see out through the cracks in the barn a small unpretentious house, white with green trim. Laying on my back and pondering the situation, I noticed a metal trolley overhead leading to an outside loft door. This was used to bring the hay up on a loading fork, pulled by a horse, attached to a suck line. I had seen the operation on the neighboring Hay plantation and it struck me as a very inventive way of raising large loads at one time and transporting them to any part of the loft. Laying there gazing at the roof, my thoughts turned to Poku, so I prayed for her to intercede for me and protect me in the event Mr. Shuman was not honest with me. Eventually I drifted off into a good sleep.

I awoke with a sudden scare, but then discovered that a dormouse must have run across my face, giving me a bit of a shock. Faint low sounding voices were coming from the outside, but the thunder was making them inaudible. As the lightening lit up the yard in front of the house, I could see four horsemen with rifles wearing black rainslickers. I said to myself that my friend Mr. Shuman was a rascal and he was figuring on spending the huge reward on my head.

Gathering up my gear, I felt for the ladder but it was gone. The varmint must have laid it on the floor below. I could see the outline of the loft door, so I felt for the wooden latch and released the catch. Peering down, I could see the glistening mud about fourteen feet below. Without hesitation, I lowered myself down the side, grasping onto the sill. Hanging on with one hand, I closed the door as much as I could and then let go, sinking into about six inches of mud and manure. I made a prompt dash away from the barn to a drainage ditch about one hundred yards away. It was more of a swale than a ditch, but it was running with knee deep water. Sloshing in four foot strides, I headed up the swale in a northeasterly direction, putting as much distance as I could between that cluster of men and myself.

After I had covered about a quarter mile, I crawled to the top of the swale and looked back to the barn. The lightening was so bright at times that it almost appeared daytime. Through the dark rain, I could see four torches moving around the outside of the barn, probably covering all exits. Eventually I could see a torch within the barn and then the light appeared in the upper half; they were in the mow looking for their quarry. Lo and behold the light became extremely bright and then I realized that they had accidentally set the mow on fire with their pine torch. They should have known that at times drops of pitch afire, drip to the ground from a burning torch, but they must know that by now, for it became a conflagration within seconds.

As I lay there watching the Shuman barn light up the rainy night sky, I thanked Poku and her little dormouse for giving me warning. In that instance, I knew that it was I who was one of God's chosen people, so I got up on my knees and gave thanks for deliverance and I also added "Thank you, little Poku."

There was a lot on my mind that eventful night as I trudged northward toward Greensboro. My thoughts ranged from the deceitful people in this world to good honest, loving men like Kweku. Then I spent the rest of the night planning my future with Jenny.

■ ■ ■ ■ ■ ■ ■ ■ ■ ■

The next few days were uneventful and very routine. My next contact, according to my map, was just on the south side of Danville. It was between Greensboro and Danville, however, that I had a life-shattering experience that I will take to my grave.

As I left my hiding place and set out at dusk, I came upon a commotion up ahead at the edge of a clearing where the woods and a cornfield meet. There was a bright three-quarter moon, so I crept as near as possible to the confrontation. From my vantage point I could see and hear everything, just as though I were part of the drama.

A group of men on horseback were in the process of hanging a young black boy of the age of sixteen, I guess. I have never in my life heard a human plead and cry for his life as that young boy. They were accusing him of being a companion of Nat Turner, a known trouble-maker. He begged them to stop, that they had the wrong man, for he did not know a person by that name. The harder he pleaded and cried for them not to kill him, the more they laughed and taunted him. I was helpless against so many, all I could do was pray and shed tears of compassion. I knew that the mother who bore him and nourished him would rather have a knife thrust through her heart than to witness such a scene.

With his hands tied behind him and the rope about his neck, they tied it to a saddle horn and hoisted him about four feet off the ground. He kicked and struggled for some time, until he finally had the life choked out of him. Had they dropped him suddenly, he would have died immediately with a broken neck, but this way he had to suffer. His body swayed for what seemed to be an hour, for he had struggled so violently. His screams still ring in my ears to this day.

When the older men had ridden off, two boys about the age of the victim stayed behind to have fun. They suggested lighting a fire beneath the body and burning it while still hanging. One red-headed boy pulled the victim's pants down and left them hanging from his feet saying that it will be like a wick.

They set about gathering firewood, stacking it beneath the hanging trousers. When they came within a few feet of my hiding place, I lunged out with great celerity and caught each of them around the throat, one in each hand. They were so startled that they made nary a sound. I had never hurt a person in my life that I could remember and I didn't mean to be so extreme, but I just froze there looking up at the young boy hanging from the limb with tears streaming down my cheeks. I could still hear his crying pleas ringing in my ears as I stood there with two limp bodies hanging from my arms.

Reality finally hit me when I realized I had killed these two young men and now I had broken a commandment. The evil thought crossed my mind to release the rope from around the young black's neck and use it to string up the two whites in his place. That would create an eerie mystery for anyone coming back to the scene, but I dismissed the urge and thought it best I move on quickly. I never even took one of the two horses standing there, for if I were caught with a stolen horse, I would also wind up a tree victim.

Moving at a fast pace, I worked my way out onto a narrow country road going to Danville. I walked in the center grass patch so I could hear any noise that might be danger. Before I got to the Virginia state line, I was startled by a voice from the side of the road. "Where are you going at this time?" It was asked in a deep resonant monotone.

"To Danville," I answered trying to make out the figure in the darkness.

"A runaway, huh?," he queried. "Don't worry. I'm in sympathy with the slaves. You're not the first one I've helped."

"Oh, thank God," I said in a grateful tone. "I need all the help I can get."

He took me off with him through the woods to a crudely constructed hut. He went inside and lighted a candle and then I entered. We sat down on a bench by a table and talked till it broke daylight. He told me he was a full-blooded Cherokee who also suffered discrimination at the hands of the white man so he retaliated by aiding and abetting runaways. I told him of my experience the evening before and of how guilt pangs had overtaken me. He laughed as though it were a joke and then he explained his rationalization. To him there is a war going on between good and evil and during war it is necessary to kill. He asked me how else I was going to stop the custom of picking up any person, accusing them of a wrong, bypassing all demands of justice, and then lynching them. He gave me a convincing argument that we had to fight back, even to the point of taking another life and then resting in peace that we had done what was best for humanity. It did ease my conscience a bit, especially when he said that I punished more than just the two young men.

"Just imagine the mystery encountered by the ones who first came upon the scene. There near the hanging victim lay two of the lynchers, with no wounds, only a bruise about the neck. Who or what could have done such a deed? To me I see it as the scales of justice being balanced," he said.

He made turkey sandwiches and sassafras tea for breakfast and then he gave me his bunk to rest on. Before he left, he showed me a trap door in the floor in case anybody were to come in. His hunting dog tied to a post in the front yard would give me plenty of warning and time to hide. He felt I would be safe from intruders. I felt comfortable enough to relax and eventually go off to sleep.

It was afternoon when he returned. He had been to town and purchased a block of cheese and soda crackers. We ate cheese, crackers and apples; it sure was delicious. He then suggested that I get prepared for my trip around Danville and on to Gretna. While he was telling me of the safest route, he cut the block of cheese in half and packed me enough food for a couple of days. To this day, I have great respect for the Cherokee people, for they all seemed to be the same, good, hard-working people who suffered unnecessarily at the hands of white invaders. I can't remember his name, for it was of Indian origin. But he was useful in directing me to Danville.

After walking about three hours I came to an intersection that baffled me. The main road went straight and the sign said Danville to the left, on what appeared to be a secondary road for there was quite a bit of vegetation growing on it. I realized that after two hours, I was in a continuous westerly direction, so I was cozened by someone who turned the road sign.

Instead of backtracking, I turned right to the north and picked my way over fences and through brush all the while bearing right. It was not until daybreak that I arrived at a marker reading 'Virginia State Line.' I should have been to the north of Danville by that time had I not been misled. I found a ditch in a wooded area that gave me cover for the day.

While trying to sleep, I did a few calculations and figured I had averaged twenty miles a day and that was with a few layovers and three days with transportation. All in all, I had escaped detection and had arrived in Virginia, so I was pleased and thanked God. At this rate, I should be in Johnstown by mid-September at the very latest, allowing for a few setbacks. My next underground station was Lynchburg, about seventy-five miles, so I figured three more days and then I'll rest and get more supplies.

That sleep was disturbed, not by a dormouse, but by a strange sensation; a stray mutt licking my face. She was a small reddish brown cross-breed with a loving face but the ugliest, wiry coat of hair I ever saw. She would cock her head to one side as though she had just asked a question and was waiting for an answer.

Reaching out and petting her, I said to her, "I'll call you Amber." She responded by licking my hand and shaking her tail. I shared some of my jerky with her and then figured I had a traveling companion whether I wanted her or not.

I wondered if Poku has sent me this stray for a reason? Is she just for companionship or is she to sound a warning and save my life? I knew that time would tell. Being a cross-breed put her in a category of a misfit, an outcast, a black slave like myself.

I was too far to the west to contact my Danville station and I had enough food to make it to Lynchburg where I would find a Mennonite underground home. I decided to move on North and not use Danville at all.

CAMBRIA TRIBUNE
Tuesday, December 18, 1860
TWELFTH DAY STORY

*A*mber and I took a northwesterly course around the little village of Gretna and made a comfortable hideaway in a hayfield that had just been windrowed. The farm was far to the west, almost out of sight, and besides, this being Sunday, I doubt anyone would be out working the hay field. It was prepared for a few days of drying. Amber crawled up on my stomach and settled down for a day's rest. She was a good walker but showed complete fatigue after an all night hike.

Keeping low until dusk, we headed north for Lynchburg. A new quarter moon came up and we found a narrow road going in our direction but no road signs. Following the road for a few miles, Amber stopped dead in her tracks and let out a low growl. I immediately hushed her and went to a ditch along the road and laid low. Sure enough, a strange scraping sound came into range and I could tell by my years of hunting that it was not a heavy object for it was dragging the surface. A heavy object would have made a deeper grinding sound.

By the light of the quarter moon, a very slender black person came into view. It was a woman just sliding her sandals along the road. She appeared too weak to lift her feet, so I stood up and stopped her when she got abreast of me. I asked her where she was going at this late hour and she responded that she had no place in mind. Then she told me her story.

She contracted consumption and was slowly dying. The plantation, whose private road we were standing on, no longer wanted her around for she was contagious. She wanted to walk until her heart gave out and maybe she could die and go to heaven. Then she asked me who I was, so I told her the story of my escape to the North.

She grabbed me fiercely by the arm and pleaded. "Oh, please. Do a dying mother one great favor and take my son with you. When I dies, he be left alone to live a life of drudgery in the cotton field. If he is free with you up north, then I can go in peace. Free to live with the angels."

"How old is your son?," I inquired.

"He be eight this coming year," she answered in her Southern dialect. "He grow fast."

"Then you mean he is just *seven* now. That is the perfect age. Poku must have sent you," I laughed.

She failed to see the humor at such a serious time so I told her how Poku was guiding me from her heavenly home and the secret code word, 'seven.'

Then she smiled and told me to wait and she went off to fetch him. Amber and I sat on a log alongside the road and pondered the situation. In just two days, Poku sent me a canine companion and a seven year old boy to take all the way to Pennsylvania. Will they be a burden or a blessing? If it is Poku's doing, it will be the latter.

After an hour's wait, the mother came shuffling up with a slender black boy whose eyes sparkled in the moonlight. He carried a small bundle in his hand.

"Dis here's Rafel, but I calls him Rafe. He's a good boy wot loves d'Lord. Take care of him please," she sobbed completely out of breath.

"Mam, I swear by our Lord in heaven that I will love him, care for him, and treat him as my very own flesh and blood. I can never have a child of my own so I'll take him to be a blessing. Now we must be off now so we can make a few miles before daylight. Say good-bye but be careful not to kiss him with your sickness."

She hugged and cried and looking upward she said, "Thank you, Lawd."

I took Rafe by the hand and said, "From now on Rafe, you can call me Daddy."

We walked in silence till daylight for I did not wish to push myself on him. I just wanted to let us grow slowly together in a more natural day by day manner. Rafe seemed to prefer that approach also for he was a strong silent type but I was anxious to find out what was going on in that little head of his. He never had a pet, so he and Amber became friends very quickly. Amber seemed to understand what was happening.

Our first day together was spent in an abandoned school house that hadn't been used for many years. Bird droppings covered the floor so it was a roosting place for birds of every description. We found a dry place where wood was stored for a little stove. If someone discovered us, we could escape through the wood door. Amber was worth her weight in gold. The smaller the dog, the more acute their hearing seemed to be, and she always warned me of any human or animal in the area by a low growl. Up to that time, I had never heard her bark. She seemed to sense that stealth was the name of our game.

While eating our first meal in the schoolhouse, I noticed that Rafe was chewing on one side of his mouth and the other appeared a bit swollen. Not until I asked did he mention that he had a toothache. I told him that if I couldn't fix it, we would have it taken care of by the Ebersole family, our next station. He had never heard of the underground railroad, so as I was explaining it to him, he drifted off to sleep.

As we walked the following evening, he asked me about my life when I was his age. He was amazed to hear that we grew up as happy children with plenty of time to swim and play. The only work we did was play to us, for we made a game of everything. Then I told him of being kidnapped at ten years of age and how life can change in a matter of minutes. His mind was very sharp and he could understand when I told him that the evil agent was 'Mr. Greed.' Rafe was very mature in mind, well beyond his seven years.

July fifteenth we arrived at a beautiful, white two-story home on the outskirts of Lynchburg. My bible insert told me to look for the special brightly colored hex sign on the fence and there it was. I could make out the name 'C. Ebersole' on the mail box. Nobody was about on that foggy morning so we went to the back door and knocked. Shortly, a man in nightcap and nightgown came to the door and let us in. He was wearing eyeglasses above a huge smile and he appeared to be in his fifties.

He said he was told a giant of a man would be by, but he hadn't heard of the boy and dog. I told him of my acquisition on the way and said only the Lord knows how large my retinue will be by the time I reach Pennsylvania.

We were led to an outkitchen attached to the house and there was a washroom that I had never seen the likes of before. He showed me how to turn the handle and the water that had been out in the sun the previous day would come pouring down over me. A bar of good homemade lye soap was given to us and we were to bathe, change clothes and be ready for a good warm breakfast.

Those Mennonite people were really great friends. They put into practice what other people preached. We were treated like paying guests and given extra clothes that were kept in a closet for runaway guests. Before each meal, a verse of the bible was read and that morning they read Psalm 63. I'll never forget it.

"Through the night watches I will meditate on you, they who seek my life shall be destroyed." That might not be exact, but that is what I remember.

Mr. Ebersole pulled the bad tooth that Rafe was enduring and gave him a medical checkup for he was well versed in home cures. He said Rafe was in better than average condition, except for an overgrown toe nail that he trimmed and put in order. Then he fitted him with his first pair of shoes, with brand new soles. Mr. Ebersole had a miniature shoe shop with every size of shoe there was. He rebuilt all old discarded shoes to be given to the poor and the likes of us.

His wife whom he called Dee, had us stay over an extra day to rest and have some good nourishing meals. She was also a nurse and a midwife besides being an excellent cook. I think that anyone who spent weeks on the road would appreciate all warm, home cooked meals. Mrs. Ebersole also renovated a large rain slicker to fit Rafe for the mountainous area ahead of us was known for its heavy rainfall. The two days we spent there were used up in preparing us for the last half of our trip. The food and clothing they gave us would take us a long way, for they warned us that after we left Forks of Buffalo, we would have some rough terrain ahead of us.

On the evening of the 17th, we bid good-bye to our gracious hosts and headed for Forks of Buffalo. It was on that leg of the journey that I knew I'd have to devise a way to carry Rafe on my back, in case I had to make a run to escape a pursuer. I had to be on the lookout for some sort of material for such a device.

Rafe's short legs had to do double work to keep up with my normal strides. I had to either slow down or take more frequent rests. Amber was enjoying herself just amblin along, but by morning she too was dog tired.

At Ledlar Mills, we stopped to rest by the mill stream and have a little lunch. As I sat on a rock and leaned against the mill shed, my back rested against a rope. There, hanging from a ring, was a rope designated for some odd purpose. It was a stout line and something that I could use to carry Rafe. I had experience in rope tying back on the scales dock, so I fashioned a Spanish bowline and then split the line so that two bights hung down my back to hold Rafe's legs and the split line came over each of my shoulders and secured down on my belt. With his legs in the loops, he could hang onto my neck and I could run without a hindrance. When we finished our meal, I had him climb into the sling and then hang on. I raced down the road and he laughed with glee for he said it was like being on top of a moving mountain. I let him dismount and then told him that in case of an emergency, or if he ever got tired, that is the method we would use.

At daybreak, it started to rain so we went deep into the woods and crawled under our ponchos. This was a new experience for both Rafe and Amber.

We took off in the rain for Buena Vista before dark and encountered steep terrain. That was the beginning of the Allegheny Mountains. Looking back, I can say that it was the most difficult part of the trip. Since the range runs Northeast to Southwest, we tried to follow a valley as long as we could. It meant crossing streams, back and forth, and getting quite wet. It was a relief when we found a logging road that took us to Buena Vista. We hid out there until dark and the rain stopped.

Our next contact with the underground was a cabin on the mountain trail to Stuart's Draft. It was a good two day walk following a well-defined trail. I never knew the woods could get so dark even with a full moon. Amber had the best scent for keeping us on the trail in the dark.

It was in the early daybreak hours that I noticed Amber's habit of running ahead and disappearing around a bend, then coming back into sight just as though she had to see that it was clear ahead of us. I truly believe that she knew that we were in constant danger and that she would let us know if trouble lay ahead.

According to my map, the Shank cabin laid off to the right of the trail going into Stuart's Draft. It was a humble log cabin owned by a hunter named Roy Shank who was a radical abolitionist. He was obsessed with the idea of freeing all humans from bondage and letting them live as free men and women in either North or South. He was a man of very few words, but took us in and gave us shelter and protection. With his collection of guns and knives, I never felt so safe and secure in all my life. His cabin was an impenetrable fortress.

Mr. Shank was my kind of outdoorsman. We shared our hunting skills, tracking techniques, and sign detection. He only laughed once and that is when I told him when I was rushed by Old Tusk and had only a stump between sure death and myself. I dug into my rucksack and showed him my kente cloth. We talked until I was too sleepy to go on, so he went outside with his pipe to stand guard while we slept until after sunset. He gave us fresh provisions and showed us a back way trail from his cabin to Staunton, practically his own private trail.

On our night journey around Staunton, we managed to find a narrow country road going up through the valley. Wanting to take advantage of an easy trail, we kept walking as the sky began to show light over the mountain. We should have taken cover at that time, but we pushed our luck.

It all seemed so peaceful and quiet as a mist rose off the valley floor when a voice from a fenced yard to our right shouted.

"Stop right where you are and don't move!"

It was then I could see an elderly man in undershirt and trousers aiming a handgun at us. I was not about to lose all I had gained so far, so I grabbed Rafe under my right arm and ran like a rabbit. Having watched the wild animals elude their pursuers, I zigged and zagged from one side of the road to the other as he fired six shots in rapid succession. I could hear bullets zinging by and I knew by my speed that I would soon be out of range and he would be out of bullets. I couldn't figure out why a man would be out with his pistol at that hour. Maybe there was something that had aroused him before we had come on the scene.

A short distance down the road we came upon a very big cattle plantation with a high stone wall running along the road. The stones were probably cleared from the field, made into a solid wall and then capped with a wide concrete top. We found the gate, which was just long wooden poles across the entrance, close enough so as to keep the calves enclosed.

Setting Rafe inside, Amber and I crossed over and walked down through the cows and their feeding calves. They appeared to be all beef cattle and a very healthy and well kept herd. Feeling in a devilish mood, we weaved ourselves through the herd that numbered in the hundreds, making 'S's all the way up through the pasture. Rafe asked the reason why and I told him to wait and see. Halfway up through the valley, I spotted a beautiful full grown hemlock tree over near the wall. Putting Rafe in his sling on my back and Amber in my front pouch, I reached up and grabbed the lower limb. Reaching hand above hand I finally was able to stand on the lower limb and walk out to the wall holding on to the upper limbs. Dismounting on the top of the wall, I set Rafe and Amber in front of me and we hastily made our way down to the end where the wall made a right angle.

It was getting quite light by that time, so I lowered Rafe down to the ground, handed Amber to him and then hit the ground myself. We made for the high ridge that loomed ahead of us as fast as we could trot. As the sun made its appearance, we arrived totally exhausted high on the ridge overlooking the beautiful lush green valley floor.

After catching our breath, I took off my rucksack and removed the bible from the rear pouch.

"My Lord and my God," I said to Rafe. "Look here at my precious bible."

There was a bullet hole through all the pages and in the final chapters of Revelations was the spent bullet. The shooter probably thought I was some sort of super human being for continuing to run after he shot me.

The 63rd Psalm came back to me: "But those who seek to destroy my life shall go down into the depths of the earth."

"Rafe," I laughed. "We are going to spend an extra day here on this mountain top just to give thanks. It will be a total day of thanksgiving." And that is exactly what we did.

Our sleep was disturbed around noon by the barking dogs. I woke up Rafe and told him to watch the hounds that the shooter had amassed to track us. The hounds entered the barred gate just as we did, and then they barked and zigzagged all through the herd, greatly annoying the nursing cows. The owners appeared on horseback with rifles and there the fun began.

When a dog got in the clear, the horseman shot it and that's the way the whole fracas went. A bitter fight ensued between the pursuers and the cattle owner for the barking dogs were scattering cows and calves in all directions. Eventually, the dogs that survived and the posse were herded back to the gate from whence they came. The dogs only got as far as the hemlock tree and then they lost our scent. Rafe and I had a good laugh and then he understood why we left our scent well dispersed about the herd.

Rafe then confided in me for the first time. He said his mother wanted him to commit his life to God so he promised to me that if we reached Pennsylvania safely, he would go into the ministry. He called me Daddy, so I responded.

"Son, that would make me the happiest man in the world. I know of no better way to live than to be a slave for Christ. Aunt Mae always said, 'True consecration to God is to find glory in drudgery.'"

CAMBRIA TRIBUNE
Friday, December 29, 1860
THIRTEENTH DAY STORY

*J*uly 23rd, 1816, was marked on my calendar as the one day of the year that we would set aside each year in thanksgiving. I explained to Rafe that had I been killed, he would have been delivered back into slavery.

On the evening of the 24th, we set out for Harrisonburg and expected to reach there just after dark. While bearing to the left to pick up our old road, we happened upon a bountiful pear tree. No doubt a hunter had dropped a pear core many years ago and this delicious fruit was the result. We filled our pouches and moved on towards our road.

It was a peaceful quiet evening and the only disruption was a lone rider who was going south. We could hear him approach off in a distance so we had plenty of time to take cover. The remainder of the night was uneventful as we circumvented Harrisonburg and headed west up the Shenandoah Mountains. It was a well used road to Rowley Springs except we would have been twice as far had the road been straight. It wound around the mountain like a serpent. Speaking of serpents, that was where Rafe encountered his first rattlesnake.

Amber was ahead of us about thirty feet when she stopped and growled in a low gurgle. It was then that I could hear the distinctive buzz of the mountain rattler. It was just telling us not to step on it. I explained that they were nocturnal just as we were, for they could not stand to be out in the hot July sun. I explained that we were now in copperhead country and they were just as bad but gave no warning.

We spent the day hiding just east of Rawley Springs and then took up our walk as the sun set, aiming northwest for the West Virginia state line. The mountains were cool and pleasant walking and as time passed, Rafe and I grew closer as father and son. I shared with him my dreams of a small cabin, just big enough for him, Jenny and myself, for the north was hostile in the winter and the smaller the cabin, the easier it was to keep warm.

Shortly after crossing into West Virginia, we descended the mountain trail and arrived at Brandywine in what we considered flat country. Those mountain trails were hard on Rafe, for by morning he said his knees ached.

As we approached Brandywine, it was near daybreak and Amber froze in her tracks and growled. I saw nothing and heard nothing out of the ordinary. I went to Amber's side and we slowly walked ahead and she led me to a large tree to the right side of the road. There she stopped and continued growling. Out from behind the tree stepped a black man and woman. I asked them where they were going, but he answered in an antagonistic manner that it was none of my business. I agreed with them and offered them some pears and only the woman took a few. If they had a problem, I thought it best that we move on and let them sort out their hostility with someone else. I never had to look for trouble; it had a habit of finding me.

Brandywine consisted of just a few houses, but I was to find one with W.C. Carroll on the gate. It was getting too light for safety but we finally found our station on the north side of town.

Mr. Carroll responded to our knock and accompanied us down a trap door in his kitchen, to a room used as a runaway station and a fruit canning cellar. He lighted two lanterns for us, showed us the wash stand and basin and told us to be ready for a hot breakfast. He was a short, gray-haired, round-faced man with a perpetual smile. He lived right with the Lord and it shone in his face. He explained that we were in unfriendly territory and we represented a year's wages for those people in the area. It was paramount that we stay in the cellar until night and then he would drive us to Fort Seybert.

We could tell by the commotion upstairs that there were many children and it was a busy household. Mr. Carroll brought down a huge breakfast of eggs, potatoes and sausage, and a large pitcher of milk, served with a half loaf of toasted buttered bread. It was a royal feast for us and the first sumptuous meal like we had last enjoyed at Ebersole's.

Mr. Carroll read us a few chapters from the book of Job just to encourage us to be tenacious and persevere and in the end we would be richly rewarded. He said the bottom line was to trust and never, never despair. He pointed to a crucifix on the wall and said, "Let Him be your example," then he went upstairs and let us sleep the rest of the day.

That evening after a meal of hot vegetable soup and roast beef, Mr. Carroll filled our rucksack with enough food for a week, then loaded us in an enclosed delivery wagon pulled by a spirited white stallion.

He originally mentioned that he would take us to Fort Seybert but when we arrived there, he said it was still early and he would take us on to Moorefield and a safe hiding place.

We reached Moorefield well before daybreak and we proceeded to the west of town to an empty silo on the bank of the south branch of the Potomac. It had been used to store ice for the summer so it was filled with a few feet of sawdust that made a nice place to bed down. The silo was quite isolated, apparently the original home and barn had burned down. Mr. Carroll sat and visited with us for a while, describing the serpentine trail north to Keyser. He figured we should be there by the 30th, two days walking. We thanked him from the depths of our hearts and he bid us good-bye, giving us his blessing and he slipped five dollars into my hand. I'll never forget Mr. Carroll.

As the day waned, Rafe called my attention to a barge tied up to the river bank. Walking about on deck was an elderly black man with a young black deck hand. In bright white letters on the bow was 'No. 7.' I just had to take a chance and contact the man on that barge. Leaving Rafe and Amber alone, I went over to the barge and boarded by way of a gangplank. I startled the elderly man and he looked up at me in dismay. Without mincing words, I explained my predicament and he agreed to help us. I made the deal a little more attractive by offering him the five dollars Mr. Carroll had given me. Then he asked me what route I had planned and I showed him my map. He sat me down and showed me that if I bypassed Keyser and stayed with him till he got up into Maryland, we could disembark when we got to the Cumberland bridge and from there go west into Cumberland, then to Meyersdale and on into the farmland of Somerset County. That would save us three days of walking and would be an enjoyable barge ride.

Retrieving my rucksack, Rafe, and Amber, we returned to the barge and settled in below deck with an assortment of cargo. The barge captain was named Sam and his helper was his son Junior. They were free men working for the barge owner from Hagerstown, Maryland, and were being given room and board and ten dollars a month. To me, that was how I visualized freedom, working for a paycheck.

Within the hour, a young drover appeared with a team of young mules. He hitched his double tree to the barge's bowline and off we went at about five miles an hour. It was sheer pleasure and we got to visit with Sam and his son as they took turns at the tiller keeping us steered off the bank. By the 29th, we would be in Maryland and that would have us cross the Pennsylvania state line the last day of July. By the third or fourth of August, I told Rafe we should be at our safe house outside of Johnstown.

Five dollars was a small fortune, but I saw it as money well spent. After dark Rafe, Amber, and I went to the offshore side of the barge where we dangled our bare feet into the nice cool water of the Potomac. We spent hours soaking our feet and admiring the passing shadows on the opposite shore. By the time it broke daylight, we pulled into the bank and tied up for a new team was to take us on north from there. Not wanting to be seen by any of the many self acclaimed bounty hunters, we stayed below deck during the daylight hours and only came out after dark to relieve ourselves and get some good fresh river air.

Due to a bit of a drought, the Maple River did not have enough water to accompany our deep draft so we thanked Captain Sam and his son and disembarked. Following the river road, we headed northwest for Cumberland in almost a light headed mood, knowing that we were so close to the Pennsylvania state line. I can't tell you how many times I repeated under my breath, "Thank you, Lord!"

We took shelter in the woods between La Vale and Cumberland waiting out the daylight hours and a light mountain rain. As soon as it would get dark, we would make a run through the hills on the old Meyersdale road, by passing Pocahontas and on to our safe house in Somerset. On my bible map it was marked as a Quaker benefactor; I had heard of those peace loving people from Aunt Mae.

The barge ride spoiled us, for we seemed out of shape for the mountainous terrain between Maryland and Pennsylvania. In my mind I had pictured it as just slightly rolling hills, but we found out differently. By the wee hours of the morning, Rafe said he was too tired to walk anymore and wanted to call it a night, but I refused to quit. I enjoyed the Pennsylvania fresh night air, after all, it was a life long dream finally being fulfilled.

I stopped to allow Rafe to slip his legs in the bights of the Spanish Bowline and with his arms about my neck, we pushed on. I could feel his hands slipping so I held them in mine; Rafe was falling asleep on my back. He weighed so little that he was easy to carry, for I had carried more weight than that in my double rucksack. Since it was just Amber and myself left awake, I sang to Amber my Jenny song, "Oh, my pretty quadroon."

We stopped at daybreak in a hayfield outside Meyersdale and were feeling safer the further north we got but at no time could we let our guard down completely for we knew from past experience, that there were some strange and greedy people out there in the world who would turn in their own mother if the price were right.

I was awakened by a strange sensation; Amber was licking my face. By the time I got my eyes open and looked about, I could see what worried Amber. The farmer who owned the field was approaching with a windrow pulled by a team of Clydesdale horses. The field was so flat and open that there was no way that we would escape without being detected.

The farmer drove directly to us and told us we were welcome to use his barn for a resting place, so I thanked him kindly and moved on toward the barn. As soon as we were far enough out of his sight, we headed for the closest wooded area. I didn't want to have another bad experience with a free offer from an unscrupulous farmer. We hid out in the woods until dark, then we took the road marked 'Somerset Pike.'

It was a night hike of about twenty miles when we reached the outskirts of the farming community of Somerset. According to my map, I should find a white farm house on Old Dutch Road, the house will have a picture of a fox on a sign hanging from a post in the front yard. We found Old Dutch Road and eventually the white farm house belonging to the Calpin family.

A shepherd dog in the front yard heralding our arrival with his loud barking, brought the residents to the door in their night clothes. We were quickly ushered in although there were no close neighbors to witness our arrival. Our hosts took us to their huge outkitchen and made us comfortable while they got dressed. Then they showed us to the washroom and had us prepare for breakfast that they would call a celebration meal to thank the Holy Spirit for our safe deliverance from South Carolina.

We preceded our five course breakfast with a prayer and then entered into a detailed conversation as to our next move. Mr. Calpin convinced me that I was reasonably safe in that area, especially from the law. Only radical bounty hunters could give me trouble, but legally, they had no jurisdiction north of the Mason-Dixon line.

When I inquired about work in the area, I was told of a humane committee that took it upon themselves to find a job and shelter for runaways. My next contact would introduce me to the committee. I inquired about work on a farm such as their hunting club and Mr. Calpin broke into laughter. He said it was no club, just a dirt poor farm that was just able to break even each year. I then inquired about the fox on the sign in the front yard and he replied that it was a secret signal that only underground people knew and it was chosen because a George Fox was the founder of the Quaker movement. Then it was my turn to laugh.

Before breakfast was finished, I was surprised to see one of the Calpin sons wheel a crippled black man into the dining room. His ebony face shone as though it were covered with oil; Aunt Mae had a similar shine to her skin. The man appeared to be about thirty years of age, with his legs terribly twisted.

Mr. Calpin said, "Ben, I want you to meet Austin who came to us over two years ago and has been the greatest blessing that this home has ever received."

The chemistry between Austin and me was perfect. He had an aura about him that any God fearing man would recognize. His body was wracked with pain but his mind and speech were sharp and clear.

He related his story to me. He was owned by a gentle man by the name of Austin Ruzicka who was talented, kind and generous but very naive. Mr. Ruzicka had a large farm in Hawkins County located in northeastern Tennessee. He had a crop failure and turned to an unscrupulous neighbor who loaned him money on a promissory note, dated just prior to harvest season. Unable to come up with the money at that time, the scoundrel Mr. Mullenix, took his farm and slaves. He was such a tyrant that we all fled to the four winds and I made it to this home. It was here that I was stricken with a paralysis and could go no further. Although I was a terrible burden, Mr. and Mrs. Calpin volunteered to let me stay on and care for me.

Mr. Calpin interrupted. "This man is the most talented, gifted person in Somerset County. He has the wisdom of Solomon and the mind of a genius. It seems as though God gave him one handicap in exchange for an outstanding mind and heart."

"Don't give me the accolades," Austin interjected. "It is God who gets the glory. I am just his hand servant."

After breakfast, I sat out on the back porch with Austin to enjoy the morning sun and basic conversation. When I referred to him as a black brother, he challenged me.

"How can you call me your black brother when you are brown?"

Before I could answer, he told me that it was very long ago that there was a black race, but it has become so diluted that the race extends from his color, to white. He thought that this was good, for it brought people together socially and caused them to realize that there is but one race nowadays, the human race. He pointed out that I was not only a mixture of Negro and Arab, but differed also from the average person by my unusual height. He explained how we were basically the same and yet unique. I could see that he had a polemic mind and was no superficial thinker. He could teach me a lot. Rafe sat and listened to Austin with great intent.

Mr. Calpin offered to drive us in his rig to the next village of Geistown where I would meet Mr. Geis and Mr, Lulay who would take me to my final destination. Before I left, I asked Austin if I could come back to visit him after I got settled and he said he would be looking forward to it. Here I will tell your readers that I visited him yearly until he died last year, January 22, 1859. He referred to my visits as my annual retreat, where I would take time off to pull back from my work and do a little self-analysis and renewal of spirit. He was my retreat master, God bless his soul.

Mr. Calpin drove us to the Geis home, situated across the road from the community cemetery. He and Mr. Lulay immediately drove us through Johnstown, up Prospect Hill and on to the village of Headrick. There, across from another cemetery, sat a very large white colonial house that was used for years by the underground railroad for those going on further north. My new hosts were the Cupancic family, not long in this country from Europe. It was the gathering place for the humane committee that came together upon the arrival of new runaways.

CAMBRIA TRIBUNE
Saturday, January 6, 1861
FOURTEENTH DAY STORY

Rafe, Amber, and I spent the night sleeping on the second story porch overlooking the cemetery. We slept as sound as our neighbors across the road.

In the morning the horses and buggies began pulling into the yard, it was a meeting of the humane society. They were all elderly men, some walked as straight as a ramrod and others were bent over from work and old age, but they were there for the sole purpose of finding me a home and a job.

Mr. Angus, Mr. Varner, Mr. Riblett, Mr. Headrick, Mr. Rosage, Mr. Benchoff, and Eddie Cupancic, our host, all met with me in the huge reception room. After proper introduction and queries as to my past work experience, Mr. John Rosage suggested that I work at the Cambria coke ovens where he has connections. Mr. Benchoff said he could spare an acre of land just about one mile from the coke ovens where I could have a home and garden with a small stream running through it. Mr. Angus had nearly one hundred acres of wooded land so he offered to cut a few trees and have them sawed at his mill to afford me a small temporary cabin, and the slash about the mill could be used to make a table, chairs, and bunks for sleeping. The others offered their farm hands as carpenters to assemble the cabin. We then loaded into the buggies and took a back trail from Headrick's, through Bingham's orchard and down to the valley floor to the Hinkston Run Road. We took the road downstream a short distance till we came to a junction where the Benchoff hill road takes off to the right.

"This bottom land will be an ideal site for Ben and his family and in proximity of his new job," said Mr. Benchoff. "We can start erecting the new cabin as soon as Mr. Angus has the lumber. I will have a steel barrel converted into a stove for warmth and for cooking."

Mr. Varner offered me a mare that had the heaves. It could not be used as a heavy dray horse, but would be perfect for short distances and light work. Mr. Headrick and Mr. Riblett offered some old harness and a well worn buggy with worn hubs that caused the wheels to wobble slightly. I thanked them all, with my eyes watering so badly that the tears dripped off my nose. This brought laughter from the rural citizens and then Mr. Rosage said he would take me directly down to my new job at Cambria Iron Works.

Rafe and Amber sat in the rear box of the buggy as Mr. Rosage drove us down to Johnstown's Cambria Iron Works. After our long trip up from South Carolina, the distance from my new home site to the coke grounds seemed like a two minute ride although it was about a mile.

The first sign of the mill to come into view was the huge pile of red, raw iron ore with the smoke belching high steel chimneys in the background. Between us and the ore piles were the bee hive shaped ovens in long neat rows contaminating the air with their putrid, eye irritating gases.

We pulled up to a wooden shack, situated by the lower tier of ovens, that served as a shelter and also as an office to keep production records. Mr. Rosage knocked at the door and it was opened by a friendly, smiling young man about my own age.

"Well, good morning, John," he greeted. "How is everything in Estherville?"

"Very good, thank you, Mike. I brought you a new hand, Mr. Ben David. Just show him how the operation functions and I'm sure he'll be the answer to the man shortage you have been mentioning. Ben, this is Mike Wingard, your new boss."

Looking up at me with a happy grin on his face, Mr. Wingard grabbed my right hand between his two hands and gave it a hardy squeeze.

"Just call me Mike," he laughed. "I am overwhelmed by your height! Maybe I didn't eat the right food when I was growing up."

I liked his sense of humor and knew that the job was going to be a pleasure.

"The pay is two dollars a day, ten hours a day with Sundays off so you can attend church. Mr. Farabaugh likes all his employees to attend the church of their choice. You'll start at seven in the morning and quit at five. You can eat while attending the ovens, so bring a lunch," Mr. Rosage instructed.

I asked him where was this place called Estherville and he pointed off to his right to a hilltop across the valley.

"That little spot on top of that hill. That's what they call that little settlement. It's really of no consequence."

He drove us back to the home site where some men were setting up property lines. Mr. Benchoff was preparing a deed description for my new home site. Mr. Rosage then drove us up the hill to the Cupancic place where he stopped to tell the men who were lingering about that I was now a bona fide Cambria employee. He wished me good fortune in my new life and departed. That was the last I ever saw of Mr. Rosage, for he worked up in the machine shop and I never had a chance to get up there. I read in the paper that he passed away at the young age of fifty-three. God bless that good man's soul.

The rest of the day was very impressionable for it was the first time since Aunt Mae gave me the bible and rucksack that I had anything of my own. My kente cloth was my first and now I had a horse, harness and wagon. The only thing absent at that time was my Jenny to share my elation.

Each day I took Rafe and Amber to work with me. Mike allowed Rafe to help carry bricks to seal up ovens that were about to be charged and also carry water to pour on the hot coke as it is removed from the ovens. We made a good working trio and when Mike's boss came around to check on us, he was pleased with our enthusiasm for work. The head boss was Mike's father, Ron Wingard. He brought me my first pay envelope after two weeks work and in it was an extra dollar for Rafe. We took one another's hands and danced in a circle, laughing with glee like a couple of three year old children. The first money I earned as a free man, no one could fully understand my joy.

Driving home that August evening with my first pay, I was in a pensive mood and left Rafe to his own thoughts. All my life I had witnessed hundreds of people who received great pleasure from beating and hurting others, there I encountered an equal number of good Christian people who risked their lives and property to help black slaves get through the underground railway. Then again, there in Headrick I found an enclave of men who went out of their way to take a total stranger, a black slave, and set him up with land, home, horse and buggy and employment. The same Christ I saw in Aunt Mae I had found in all those people who helped me get from the Jowers place to my own piece of earth at the foot of

Benshoff hill along Hinkston run. Poku, with God's help, was taking good care of me. Mike said the man I replaced always started at eight in the morning but John Rosage specified that I start at *seven*. That was Poku intervening. After three weeks with the Cupancic family, Rafe, Amber, and I moved into our own little plantation home on Hinkston run. I spent my daylight hours after work teaching Rafe reading, arithmetic, and the block writing that I knew. He was a smart and industrious boy who was most interested in what the bible had to say. We burned a lot of tallow after dark studying the letters of Saint Paul.

Our Sundays were spent visiting new found friends after church in Cambria city where Mike and his wife attended St. Mary's. With our horse and buggy, we covered the area from Wesley Chapel to Johnstown, all over Benchoff hill and all the way down to Mineral Point to see the river and go through a coal mine.

One Sunday afternoon while visiting Mr. Headrick, I noticed the red slick clay that he had excavated when he dug his basement. It was the purest clay I had seen in all my travels, free of stones or gravel. When I asked permission to load some in my wagon, he said he was glad to get rid of the whole pile. Rafe and I took a load home and we rationalized that this was not desecrating the Sabbath for it was strictly a fun experiment.

Reaching home, we took our clay to the edge of Hinkston run and there, mixing the clay with water to make it pliable, we put the supple clay in a wooden form twelve inches by six inches by six inches. We made six of these forms and before dark, we raised the forms and exposed the six clay blocks.

The following foggy September morning we arose at daybreak and with our lunches in the wagon we hitched Maude up and went to see how firm our clay blocks had set. They appeared good and firm, so we loaded them into our rig and headed for the coke plant.

We opened an oven that was scheduled to be emptied that Monday and pulled out the coke and smothered it with water. When we had all the coke out, I put my clay blocks into the oven and placed a few brick in the opening so as to preserve the heat. When Mike came to work at seven, he found us busy hauling the fine coal and bricks to prepare a new oven. When we explained why we were at work so early, he thought that it was an ideal way to use the heat that would normally be wasted.

By quitting time, our clay bricks were too hot to handle, so we decided to let them bake for another day. We couldn't use the hive for coke until it cooled off anyway.

We were so pleased with our project that we made more forms and made more clay blanks. I knew that before Sunday I would have to make a trip up to Headrick and get another load of clay. Eventually I was making two trips a week.

The clay bricks sounded like a high pitched bell when I struck them with a piece of metal. They were the finest homemade bricks in Cambria County as far as Rafe and I were concerned. Rafe got the idea of making a brand of heavy wire and stamping each brick with the initials 'B&R' since we were like two real business men.

Our brick enterprise grew until we had to shut it down for the cold weather made our clay too hard to work. We were undaunted, and left our supply of bricks stacked next to our future foundation and turned our efforts to making box traps for the abundant supply of rabbits in the area. The first frost kills off the worms that plague the rabbits, so they become a good source of meat during the cold weather. I showed Rafe how we made the trap back in the Gold Coast when Kweku and I were hunting wart hogs.

The days were short during the winter, so we went to work in the dark. It was warm around the ovens and we were willing to forego a little discomfort for the money. We bought our supplies in Cambria City that stayed open for the mill workers until six o'clock in the evening. I also had to buy feed for Maude through the harsh winter months. We didn't complain for our shack was warm and cozy with the wood heat and we had enough to eat. We were blessed by the Lord, for our cup was running over.

Our first Christmas was the ultimate of holidays and could not have been better. I bought Rafe a sheep-skin lined coat and gloves and he made me an intricately carved cross made from a single piece of pine with a beautiful brown knot at the intersection of the vertical and horizontal pieces. It was so well planned that the graduated circles could be interpreted to mean that from this very center everything grows. It was very meaningful to me and I was able to draw a great lesson from it.

We received many invitations for meals with friends that day, reminding me how blessed I was to have so many caring people, considering I had just been in the area only five months. The Knable family stopped by with a roasted chicken, stuffing, potatoes and gravy. Since we were going out for dinner and supper, we put the food in our outside window box to be eaten at a later date. They inquired about Rafe's schooling and I explained that I was giving him some home teaching. They suggested that I enroll him at the parochial school that their children attend, for it would be no imposition for them to pick him up every day as they went by our place to school. Rafe was excited about his schooling so I enrolled him for the first of the year.

Rafe's schooling had its ups and downs, for he was the only black child in an all-white school. The first lesson he learned was that some children can be as cruel as adults simply because of ignorance. It was difficult for Rafe, but an understanding teacher took him under her wing and guided him through the traumatic experience.

As for Rafe's scholastic abilities, he was recognized to be very intelligent, but had to be shifted from grade to grade depending on the subject. By June, he was promoted to the fourth grade where he resumed his studies in September.

CAMBRIA TRIBUNE
Wednesday, January 10, 1861
FIFTEENTH DAY STORY

With the help of friends and neighbors, my new brick cabin took shape. The blocks were laid as fast as Rafe and I could produce them, so at that speed we had all the walls up and chimney erected by July 1st. Then we had just the roof, front and back porches to finish.

To celebrate Independence Day, most of the mill employees were given the week off. This was a rare event. I took advantage of the holiday by visiting my mentor in Somerset County, Austin Ruzicka. I was encouraged to make that retreat by the local doctor who had a hobby of renovating buggies and light wagons. He not only offered to rebuild my worn wheels, but also loaned me his sleek Tennessee Walker and doctor's wagon, that in reality is a very light buggy. Dr. John Wolf had heard about my struggle to get started with my new life through the humane committee.

Rafe and I got an early morning start and passed through Johnstown before the town came awake. With that sleek fast stepping horse and fancy buggy, I felt like a plantation owner. The hill up through Geistown was no hindrance or obstacle for that mare. She took us to the Calpin place by high noon.

We were given the royal treatment and were accepted as honored guests of Austin. His face beamed as he greeted us and that made me feel ten feet tall for here was a man with such a brilliant mind happy to see a plain common ordinary laborer.

The main reason for that visit was a problem that would not go away; the strangulation of those two white men back at the lynching site. A guilt complex nibbled at me every day since the accident occurred. I call it an accident because I had no time for reflection on the act before it took place and I did not have full consent of my will.

Austin assured me that I would not be held responsible before God because of my irrational mood at that time. Since God forgave Moses and David for their killings, Austin figured His mercy would be extended to me also. My confession of guilt to Austin was like a thousand pound weight lifted from my shoulders.

On my arrival back to our partially finished home, I was shocked to find a letter tacked to the door of our shack. It was from Aunt Mae addressed to Mr. Cupancic. Inside the envelope were two letters; one from Aunt Mae and one from Jenny. Aunt Mae's letter read as follows:

"*My dear friend,*

I was so elated to hear of your arrival in Johnstown, for you gave me an awful scare when you failed to report in at Danville. When I received a notice from Mr. Ebersole that B&R had arrived and were safely dispatched, then I assumed that you picked up a traveling companion.

Jenny and Kweku attend my classes as often as they possibly can and I am happy to report that they are both excellent students. Jenny's accompanying letter will attest to that.

Be a good boy, Ben, and remember to help all others as best you can and together we'll make this a better world."

Love, Aunt Mae.

Dearest Ben,

Kweku and I miss you terribly, but we hope to remedy that shortly. Aunt Mae told us of your safe arrival in the North and your cousin and I hope to have the same good fortune next year.

Mr. Hay has married a German lady named Helga but she cannot adapt to this humid climate here in South Carolina. They have plans to move to the island of Bermuda after selling this plantation. The place is now up for sale and Jowers wants to buy it. Mr. Ron is hoping for a different buyer for he does not approve of the way Jowers treats his slaves.

Mr. Ron has told us that he will give us all a certificate of freemen and one hundred dollars each as starter money to begin a life of our own choosing.

As soon as this place is sold, Kweku and I will be joining you in the north. Please write to Mrs. Helga Hay and let her know exactly how we can find you in such a large area.

I am beholding to Aunt Mae who helped me write this letter and paid for postage.

All my love to you, dearest Ben. With God's help we will be together in the year 1818. Good-bye for now, sweetheart.

Your betrothed, Jenny"

Only the Good Lord can remember how many times I read that letter, over and over again. I came to memorize it word for word by copying the writing for I wanted to get away from block writing to script writing like the educated white folks do.

When I returned the buggy and mare to Dr. Wolf and picked up Maude and my rebuilt buggy, I had to tell him that my wife to be would be joining me the following year. He joined me in my state of delight and said that he wanted to host the wedding when the marriage took place.

Rafe couldn't quite understand my personality change for I believe he mistook my responding as sort of a reversion to my childhood. I explained to him that he would be getting a new mother who could provide for him a quality that was beyond my ability. This new mother could not replace his birth mother, but she could fill a void that every young boy should have. He would be ten years old and could be taught to cook and do house chores properly, not like I was doing. He conceded that the future did look much brighter.

From the day I received the letter, I worked at a furious pace getting the house finished to where it would be called "our home." The furniture had to be made, a decent barn built and enough money saved to buy a new horse. Maude was breathing heavier by the day and her heaves were getting worse.

The winter of 1817 and the spring of 1818 were mild enough to get much accomplished. I wanted to have the place looking proper for a queen but I know Jenny would accept what I could do as my best.

On the wall I hung my kente cloth and on another wall I made a frame and holder to display the bullet I removed from my bible. They looked like precious souvenirs on my newly white-washed walls. Rafe asked if he could hang a picture of spring flowers he had painted in school just to add color. I knew he was very proud of his painting.

June 7th was the date on my next letter from Jenny via Aunt Mae. It overflowed with ecstasy for the plantation had been sold and Mr. Hay not only issued all hands their freeman certificates, but gave them their one hundred dollars seed money. Kweku and Jenny were offered transportation on the dray wagons hauling Hay's valuable furniture and possessions to Charleston. From Charleston they were taking a ship to Philadelphia and then overland by the way of the Philadelphia-Lancaster Pike. From Lancaster they planned to take the stage on the Forbes Trail exiting at Somerset County.

Rafe and I held our standard celebration dance by holding hands and jumping up and down while going round and round.

I fixed up a bed for Rafe in the kitchen and reserved the extra long double bed for Jenny and me in the bedroom. My head boss's wife, Mrs. Linda Wingard, volunteered to help me buy the necessary utensils for the kitchen that I wanted to be a special treat for Jenny. All the labor saving devices I could afford, I bought. The outstanding appliance was a copper washing machine that tumbled back and forth by means of a handle swung back and forth by the operator. Attached to the adjoining tub was a hand operated set of rubber rollers used to wring out the wet clothes. I was happy with our home and felt prepared to greet Jenny.

The weeks went by very slowly as Rafe and I awaited our loved ones from the south. We spent our Sunday evenings on the front porch and as I reminisced about my youth at home and then on the Gold Coast, Rafe sat as in rapture listening to my life unfold. I would reassure him

that at the end of my rainbow it was not a pot of gold but
something much more valuable, my Jenny.

August 31st, just before quitting time, I was working on
the top tier preparing to change one of the ovens, when I
noticed Mr. Mike waving, beckoning me to come down to
the shack where he was conversing with a boy mounted on
a nervous steed. He was a messenger from the stage depot
who was reporting guests had arrived for Mr. Ben David
who was employed at the coke ovens.

Mr. Mike suggested that we close up for the day and he
would bring his rig along to help me take my guests and
luggage to my place.

When we arrived at the depot on Market Street, there
stood my big, tall, handsome cousin in the first fancy attire
I had ever seen him wear and standing at his side was a
long-skirted beauty with a white fancy bonnet framing her
light chocolate face. What a beauty to behold! I jumped
from the wagon without tying up Sugar Babe; Rafe grabbed
the reins to hold her steady. I swept up Jenny in the crook
of my left arm and hugged Kweku with my right arm. God
could not have delivered me a better pair.

After the proper introduction, we loaded all the gear in
my wagon and Mr. Mike drove my rig. My loved ones sat
in Mr. Mike's buggy for it was a much fancier rig. So with
Jenny by my side and Kweku and Rafe in the rear seat, we
headed around the mill and up the Hinkston Run Road.

Jenny fell in love with my home-made house, referring
to is as our love nest. Kweku was amazed at the progress I
had made since leaving the Jowers place. We stayed up
late into the night for Mr. Mike said he would give me the
following day off and find a helper to take my place. We
talked well past midnight.

Rafe gave his bed to Jenny and made himself a bed on
the floor of our bedroom. Kweku and I slept in the big bed.

After breakfast, Jenny and I went to Cambria City to see the priest about our wedding. He set the date for September 7th, so I got word to Dr. Wolf.

It is hard for me to remember every detail and who all were there for I had never been to such a large gathering before. The wedding was held at St. Mary's and the reception at the church hall. There were between fifty to sixty people there and Dr. Wolf provided a bountiful meal. The bride was the center of attention for with her beautiful dark skin, ebony glistening hair in her pure white gown, she was an angel to behold. I remember asking myself what I had ever done to deserve such a beautiful wife.

Kweku, who changed his name to Ron Hay, took my place at the coke plant for a week while Jenny and I went off for a honeymoon. Dr. Wolf had a summer cabin alongside a lake at Galitzin. We only stopped talking while we slept and then Jenny said she heard me say another girl's name, 'Poku.'

We returned to our little home on Hinkston Run to join Rafe and my new cousin Ron. It was a sad day for while I was away, Amber died in Rafe's arms. I had to retreat to the backyard for a few hours to spend time with my faithful companion who helped to bring me safely to the promised land. We had been through a lot together so our parting was a great shock to me.

Kweku went to Ebensburg to have his name changed legally to Ron Hay and while there, happened to hear from a friendly citizen that the old Lauer place was for sale in Carrolltown. It was to be sold for the taxes due which amounted to almost five hundred dollars. Between Kweku, Jenny and myself, we came up with three hundred and seventy five, and the rest we borrowed from George Angus, a good-hearted Christian. My cousin took possession of his first bit of earthly goods and I didn't hear from him for over a year for he worked constantly on his potato farm.

Rafe worked hard during the summer months and during school days. He excelled in his studies.

Harmony reigned at our little house despite the fact that Jenny and I could never have children as natural birth parents. Jowers' henchmen's brutality went so far that it even reached Jenny, for she so much wanted an infant to cradle in her arms.

As the years slipped by, Rafe went on to secondary school and despite his good grades, he was still searching for something more. Father Wittbrod, who married us, told Rafe of an abbey at Latrobe that could give him the education he was seeking and maybe discover his vocation in the process.

We packed Rafe's clothes and homemade trinkets and sadly sent Rafe off with Father Joe to his new life at St. Vincent's monastery. It was a day's journey of about thirty miles so we packed a good nourishing lunch for the two of them. Rafe appeared exhilarated, just as though he was fulfilling a life long dream.

CAMBRIA TRIBUNE
Tuesday, January 16, 1861
THE FINAL STORY

June 15, 1828, was a red letter day in our life as free black folks. Our son Rafe was ordained at the Benedictine Monastery at Latrobe and Jenny and I were invited to attend the ceremony. Father Joe Wittbrod took us to the huge stone school in the rolling hills where the chapel stood as an anchor to the complex.

Rafe stood out among the other four white seminarians in his white alb with a smile that went from ear to ear. As the five of them lay on the floor, prostrate before Bishop Wirtner, it reminded me of our slave days when we were humiliated before our masters. At the ordination it was a case of submission before our God, that those men would be slaves and servants to their Creator. I thought to myself at the time, "Man's desire to be God was the trouble in the South."

After the ceremony, we drove back to Cambria City and on June 16th Rafe said his first Mass at St. Mary's church and Jenny and I were his first communicants. I told Rafe that his mother was looking down on him and Jenny and I were proxy for her at the communion rail. Tears filled his eyes as he remembered the night his mother gave him over to me. I had done my best as I had promised her so I looked up to heaven and said to myself, "It is consummated." Rafe told the story of his mother in his homily at that first mass.

Rafe took the full name of Father Raphael David and went on to be a Benedictine missionary, serving a few years at Carrolltown with his cousin Ron Hay in the congregation.

We managed to visit Ron once every year, mostly in the fall when we could bring back a year's supply of potatoes for our bin. Ron prospered and was able to become a well known benefactor at the County children's home. God had blessed him so he said he wanted to share his blessings. Each year when he butchered a hog, he would remind me of our escapade with the wild boar in the forest near our Asante village. He took to the tree and left me with a stump!

My job at the mill was changed to the furnace area where the heat was the greatest hazard. It was an advancement as far as pay was concerned and I got more days off. I only worked for eight hours and five days a week, for the heat at times was more than a human could endure. I had the job filling the molds making pig iron ingots and oft times my clothes smoked and would nearly burst into flame.

In May 1852, the furnaces were shut down for the company was working on a process to produce a more refined type of steel. The shutdown would include the time to let the furnaces cool down so the changes could be made. Jenny and I planned to use this time to expand our brick business. The company allowed me to use the open coke hives while they cooled, to make the bricks that I sold to earn extra money. It was at this break period that we decided to upgrade the business.

A fabricating plant in York advertised slip forms for making bricks in just a fraction of the time, so we decided to investigate them. That was our first vacation since our honeymoon thirty-four years ago.

Mr. Knable took us to the Railroad Street station where the canal boats were pulled from the basin and loaded on railroad cars. We were assigned to a small boat named Kittanning #7, painted in a bright canary yellow with green trim. Our quarters were in the bow section where two other couples and the captain were housed. The stern half of the boat housed a couple with five children and the company chamber maid.

That trip was my second encounter with prejudice in an open confrontation. A certain Mr. Parsons, who was a husky overweight drover, had a problem with black people. Very quickly, and in no uncertain terms, he let us know that we were not welcome as traveling companions. When he used the appellation "You and your harlot," I said it would be most appropriate if we were to step out on the deck and discuss the matter as gentlemen. My anger was showing in my eyes when the Captain requested that Mr. and Mrs. Parsons transfer to the stern section. I'm sure that they didn't consider the five children as proper companions either, for they tried to disembark in Mineral Point but reboarded at the last minute.

My first encounter with prejudice occurred just across the run from my home. I had the job of going down into the valve recess and turning off the furnace water supply when it was requested by the company. One day while working on the valve, two young men who were out hunting came upon me. Only one carried a hunting gun, but these two were hunting for trouble more than small game. Just my head stuck above ground as I stooped to turn the valve.

"Well, well, what do we have here? A darkie who probably has a bounty on his head." He poked the gun in my face as he spoke.

I raised up to my full height and climbed out of the pit. When I stood over the two I could sense a sudden grip of fear, for they were overtaken by my size. The one who was armed thought the gun was a great equalizer for he kept it aimed at my stomach. I grabbed the barrel in my left hand pushing it clear of my body and the gun shot off near my ear. The hunter screamed in agony, for I had broken his finger caught in the trigger guard. They both took off for the hill, leaving me standing there with this scatter gun. It now hangs on my living room wall.

Getting back to our trip on the Portage Railroad, it was slow going from the canal basin up to the Portage Tunnel. There we were winched up to the Tunnel grade and rehitched up to the mules. The dark tunnel was approximately nine hundred feet long and smelled of manure and dampness.

Our first rest stop was at Mineral Point and there we rested before crossing the Conemaugh Viaduct, a great stone bridge. We slowly proceeded up to Portage, Lily, and finally winched up to the summit at Cresson and the gray stone Lemon House.

We had a rest and refreshments at the Lemon House where Mr. Parsons gave me a wide berth. He just seethed with hatred, so he was unable to enjoy such a wonderful experience.

Our run down beneath the skew bridge and down the mountain to Hollidaysburg was a once in a lifetime experience. Captain Shank told us of his undergoing a traumatic ride down the mountain in a runaway, when the rope broke. That was before they started using the safety car device behind the wheels.

We transferred from the flatcar to the canal at Hollidaysburg and reattached to the stern section. A team of mules took our bow line in tow and we traversed the Pennsylvania Main Line in serene comfort. The chambermaid took good care of us and set up our table and bunks in good order. Jenny took her turn at the stove, cooking me good Cajun food.

Our boat took us across the main line till we came to the Susquehanna river where we traveled southeast on the river, courtesy of the Codorus Navigation System. Shortly after passing the Union Canal to Reading, we turned right and took the short spur to York. All in all it was a wonderful experience.

York was a farming town of neat, clean houses and shops. The people were different than in Johnstown, for most were Amish, Mennonite and Dunkards and dressed in plain colorless clothes. They were polite but very reserved, so when we went to the factory to view the brick molds, the men were sincere and courteous. They demonstrated how swiftly a mold could be filled and then released in a very short time, leaving the brick unscathed. We bought the molds for forty brick and had them disassembled and packaged for shipment on our barge back home.

Jenny and I took the afternoon off to do some sightseeing and visit the shops. I told her that the first word I had learned in English was 'YORK' because it was printed on all the machinery back on the Jowers plantation.

Call it a coincidence or whatever you may, but as I had just finished telling of my first learning lesson, we were headed across the cobblestone street to a millinery store. Stepping off the curb, in fancy southern clothes, was a short fat man with a wisp of red hair. I looked at him and he glared back at me in recognition. Then it also hit me, it was Ashley Jowers there in York at the same time as myself. As we got within two feet of each other, he pulled a derringer from his waistband and screamed, "You cur!" I brushed aside his arm and the gun fired into the canopy of a passing buggy. I landed full weight upon him, crashing his body to the cobblestone. He made a gasping sound and laid still with his eyes rolled back in his head.

Jenny grabbed me to help me to my feet and a crowd of Amish people gathered around. The town constable was summoned and he told me I was in his custody. Then he took down names and statements from the witnesses and a doctor was called to the scene. Ashley Jowers was pronounced dead. Death by a crushed skull was the verdict.

I was taken by police wagon to the station and Jenny was allowed to accompany us. After questioning and taking my statement, I was asked to remain in York an extra day, then released on my own recognizance.

A municipal judge heard my story and that of witnesses and I was released and completely exonerated of any wrong doing. I told the judge that I felt terrible and wished it hadn't happened, but he said "Considering the alternative, self-preservation is a natural instinct." The constable offered to turn the derringer over to me, but I would not accept it. The scattergun and the bullet displayed on my wall was enough evidence that a young girl in heaven named Poku, with the help of God, was taking care of me.

Jenny and I returned to our home to live in peace.

To the readers of this biography, I would like to add that I would not be here to tell this story today if it were not for all those good people who live according to their Christian principles. They gave, that I might survive, so I will be eternally grateful to them. Thank you one and all.

Editor's Note: The names of the underground participants have been changed for their own protection and the events scrambled so that no harm may come to them. God bless them.

–Jack Zane

■ ■ ■ ■ ■ ■ ■ ■ ■